Mr. Beans

Dayton O. Hyde

Boyds Mills Press

Published by Caroline House
Boyds Mills Press, Inc.
A Highlights Company
815 Church Street
Honesdale, Pennsylvania 18431
Printed in The United States of America

U.S. Cataloging-in-Publication Data
   (Library of Congress Standards)

Hyde, Dayton O.
     Mr. Beans / by Dayton O. Hyde. — 1st ed.
  [160]p. :   cm.
Summary: A boy rescues a performing bear in this story of high
adventure.
  ISBN 1-56397-866-0
  1. Adventure and adventurers — Fiction. 2. Bears — Fiction.
  I. Title.
     [F] 21   2000   CIP   AC
  99-69852

First edition, 2000
The text of this book is set in 12-point Usherwood Medium.

10 9 8 7 6 5 4 3 2 1

For my daughter Ginny,
who has patiently listened to my stories
before the Yamsi fireplace

—D. O. H.

One

THE INDIAN BOY'S NAME was Robert Butterfly, but one day he was playing at the edge of a small Oregon town with a white kid named Mugsy Flanigan, and Mugsy started calling him Chirping Bird. The name stuck like chewing gum to the bottom of a church pew. Mugsy had a thing about nicknames; if a kid didn't have one, he dished one out pronto, the sillier the better.

Mugsy's own first name was Algernon. One of the smaller kids on his block tried calling him that once and ended up with the tip of his nose pointed toward the south corner of his left eye. Mugsy he stayed.

He palled around with Chirp because the Indian boy was new in town and the only one who would tolerate him. Mugsy's choice of an Indian for a friend drove the white boy's father up the wall; it wasn't that his old man had lost a great-grandfather in the Indian wars or anything like that. The man was just a snob.

Mugsy and Chirp were playing Indian one day at the edge of a pine forest just outside of town when it happened, when the idea popped into Alger-oops-Mugsy's head that was to spoil their friendship and change Chirping Bird's life forever.

Chirp and Mugsy had built a splendid tipi of poles and pine boughs and were planning to camp out for the night. Chirp had done most of the work, while Mugsy, true to form, had settled down comfortably with his back against a rotting pine log and bossed.

"I'm fourteen to your thirteen," Mugsy declared, "which gives me the right to be headman. And if I'm going to be chief, I gotta have me an Indian. Right?"

Chirp shrugged and said nothing. Being the lone Indian kid in an otherwise white community, Chirping Bird was too shy to make many friends. Mugsy was red-haired, brash, and a bully, and his thinking some days was about half a bubble off plumb. Chirp accepted him because there was no one else. Besides, he had no desire to be chief if that meant sitting around camp on his duff giving orders.

Loafing around, Mugsy had stayed clean, while Chirp, covered with pitch bleeding from the pine boughs, looked unkempt.

"You look as though you just finished a romp in the pen of a pig!" Mugsy said. "Go comb your hair. You got so many pine needles stuck on you some bird's going to want you for a nest."

Chirp made a rough pass through his long black hair with his fingers, scraped a blob of fresh pitch off his buckskin jacket, and went on with his work. Carefully intertwined with poles to make up the tipi's walls, the pine boughs gave off a clean, heady odor, almost overpowering at times. The boy lined the floor with sagebrush leaves, then dragged in another load of boughs and made Mugsy and himself each a bed. For a moment he thought to cheat a little and save some of the softest boughs for himself, but he felt the chief's critical eye on him and gave Mugsy the best.

In the gloom a mosquito hummed about, exploring the walls. Mugsy pawed the air and slapped the side of his cheek, leaving a smear of blood where another mosquito had been feeding. His enthusiasm for camping out was fading fast.

Chirp looked about the tipi, frowning. "We forgot to leave a smoke hole at the top where the poles come together," he said. "That way we could have a nice fire and the smoke would have kept the darn skeeters from getting drunk on type O."

"Who cares about dumb old skeeters?" Mugsy said bravely. "Your ancestors lived in the woods with them all the time and didn't give doodly-squat about them. I suppose they just covered themselves with pine pitch till only their eyes showed. Just like you! A mosquito tries to bite through that rind of pitch you're wearin' and it'd put a U-bend in its needle for sure."

The mosquitoes seemed to sense his arrogance

and droned about his head. Mugsy grabbed a pine branch and swatted wildly, but they only returned in force. He tried lying down on his bed and covering himself with some of the boughs. The gathering darkness seemed to bring legions of mosquitoes out of the neighboring swamp. He leaped to his feet, striking out angrily. Tripping on the anchor rope, which ran from the apex down to the floor, he almost brought the walls down around them.

"Aw, who cares?" Mugsy said. "It's just a pile of pine branches. And who wants to lie here all night getting skeeter bit? Not me!" He crawled out the door, pulling his denim jacket over his head against the bugs.

In a moment he was out of the forest, leaving Chirp to follow. It was still early, with plenty of cars on the streets. "Let's do somethin'," he said. "Our folks'll think we're camped out. They'll never check."

"Do something? Like what?" Chirp asked, catching up.

Mugsy frowned and slowed down as though the whole process of serious thought was tough going. "I got an idea," he said, perking up. "I'd still like to play Indian. Let's go count coup the way the old Indians used to do."

"Count what?" Chirp asked, a bit puzzled. But he was all ears. Mugsy had read some books and really did seem to know a lot about Indians, though he sure could have helped Chirp remember to put a smoke hole in the roof of that tipi. He trotted to catch up with the older boy, who had suddenly taken off and was headed down a darkened street toward the main part of town.

Mugsy was chattering away about Indians and Chirp didn't want to miss a chance to hear about his ancestors. He wanted to be an archaeologist some day and was starving to know his roots, but Chirp's foster parents were part white and didn't seem to want to be reminded of their Indian origins. What he had learned, he had gleaned either from his Uncle Frank, who now lived way up in Idaho, or from Mugsy.

"C'mon, Mugs. What were you talking about? Say it again. You talk like you're sucking on a mouthful of marbles."

"I said 'Let's go count coup,' you freak," Mugsy snapped, squashing a mosquito on his swollen forehead. "My Uncle Buck used to live with Indians back in Montana or somewhere. Said when an Indian wanted to prove to the other Indians how brave he was, he'd take a stick or lance or somethin', git on his old war pony, gallop straight into the enemy's camp yellin' bloody murder, and touch the meanest, toughest Indian there with his stick. Not kill 'im, mind you. Just touch him, like on the chest. And then he'd make tracks out of there afore he took on so many arrows he'd look like a porcupine."

"You mean that?" Chirp asked delightedly, trying to picture it all. "You suppose Indians really did that?"

"Or he'd go crawlin' on his belly into the

9

enemy's camp in the dead of night and steal the chief's favorite horse where it was tied right beside his lodge. Somethin' bogglin' like that, and when he got back to his camp his tribe would have a big powwow and give him horses and the hand of his own chief's daughter, who would scratch his back for him and mend his moccasins. Chiefs lost a lot of horses and daughters that way."

Chirp staggered along behind, intoxicated by a daydream. There was that Kathryn Anne Weidman who always got off at the first stop of the school bus. Not that he'd ever dared talk to her, but wow! His thoughts soared. He had just counted coup, done something really brave, and her parents were insisting that he take Kathryn Anne's hand in marriage. "Really, folks, it was nothing!"

Mugsy's voice dragged him back to reality. "Git on up here, Chirpo, where I can talk to you and get some ideas."

The boy trotted to catch up. "Hey," he said, getting into the spirit of the adventure. "Old Man Gogarn keeps a workhorse for dragging in firewood. Pastures it on his back forty. Maybe we could sit in a tree and jump down on its back when it comes in to stand in the shade." He fingered the buckskin medicine bag around his neck as though it might further inspire him. Uncle Frank had given it to him when he'd left for Idaho, telling him it had belonged to an ancestor.

"Aw, you'd fall off and break your fool neck," Mugsy scoffed. "And me, when I get near a horse, I get asthma." He stopped in his tracks as faint strains of band music came wafting in like mill smoke in the evening air. "Hey," he said. "You hear that music? It's comin' from Diamond Sally's!"

"Diamond Sally's! Howja know that?"

"I been there. Lotsa times."

"You've been in that place? You've seen her in person?"

"Of course. And what's more, I saw her do her dance onstage with her pet grizzly bear."

"No fooling! You saw her? Diamond Sally? And you saw the bear?"

"There she was up on that stage, dancin' up a storm, an' that big bear twirlin' round and round her. Must have been ten feet tall!"

"G'wan, you never saw her! Your age they'd never let you in the front door. They serve booze there."

"Nobody said I went through the front door. I snuck over the fence into kind of a courtyard where they keep the bear in a big iron cage, an' the back door to the place was wide open."

"Boy!" Chirp exclaimed. "Would I ever like to see that! The bear I mean." He glanced at the older boy shyly. "And Miss Sally, how'd she look? Guess she must be the most beautiful woman in the whole world!"

"Kinda fat. She had a diamond in her belly button big as that!"

"No!" Chirp giggled. "Not in her belly button!" He sagged against the bole of an elm tree, out of control.

"In her belly button," Mugsy repeated, pleased with his audience. "You better get away from that tree. You're liable to get Dutch elm disease and your nose will fall off."

"Belly button! Belly button!" Chirp choked. "Tell me some more!"

"I didn't get time to see her face. I had to get out of there fast. I peeked around the curtains and there was my old man in the front row."

Mugsy stopped suddenly in the middle of the street, whapping his tangle of red hair with his fist. "I got it! I got an idea! We'll count coup on the bear! We'll build ourselves a coup stick with feathers tied to it, and when no one's around, we'll sneak up to the bear's cage, reach in through the bars to count coup on him, then run like hell."

"Fishfeathers!" Chirp said, suddenly becoming thoughtful. "You call that being brave? He can't hurt you in that cage. 'Sides that, he's plumb gent-le. That picture in front of the club shows Miss Sally giving the bear a big hug. I saw a grizzly once in a zoo. He was really tame. I fed him a whole bag of peanuts."

"But did you touch him?" Mugsy snapped, becoming irritated. "Anybody can throw food in through the bars. C'mon. Honest Injun. Did you really touch him? Tell me the truth."

"Well, no," Chirp admitted, thinking back and picturing the bear. Maybe Mugsy was onto something! Boy, was that bear ever huge. And kind of scary, too. Like when he'd run out of peanuts, the animal stood up on his hind legs and looked him over, slobbering up froth. His Uncle Frank said he slobbered because they might have pulled out all his teeth to keep him from biting people and now he had trouble chewing. Chirp had been struck by a sudden vision of the bear swimming the moat and climbing right over the bars and had suddenly found things to do elsewhere, like watching the porcupines sleep.

"C'mon," Mugsy said with a sudden burst of resolve. "I saw a dead flicker in the park today. We'll take some feathers, tie them to a willow stick, then we'll sneak into the compound and count coup on that bear."

Chirp was still uncertain. "Let's not and say we did," he said. "Maybe we ought to let that bear alone."

"You're chicken!" Mugsy taunted.

"Ain't!"

"Are too!"

"Ain't!"

"Well, that settles it then. Let's go find that dead bird."

In the yellow light of a street lamp, Mugsy took out his pocketknife, slipped up to a willow tree, and cut himself a wand. Within moments he had peeled off the bark, exposing the gleaming white wood, and started on his way, leaving Chirp to follow or stay.

For a long moment, Chirping Bird stood looking about him, at the sleeping buildings gloomy with night, and wished they had stayed in the woods in that little glade amongst the pines. Then with a sigh of resignation, he turned and caught up with his friend.

Two

SOME PROWLING PREDATOR in search of a night's meal had found the dead flicker and eaten it, but there were enough salmon-red tail feathers still lying about to decorate Mugsy's coup stick. He bound the stiff feathers with a leather thong from his boot, then dangled them from the willow stick.

"There," he said, poking Chirp in the chest with the stick. "That thing looks Indian. Now we gotta go do our thing without being eaten by the bear."

Chirp's eyelids were already itchy with fatigue, but he tagged along as the older boy climbed over a weathered wooden fence and took a shortcut down a darkened alley.

They heard a rumble as a truck turned a corner and headed their way. "Hold up a minute," Mugsy commanded. "Wait till that produce truck has gone by before you cross the street. We don't want to get

15

picked up in those headlights. Somebody just might ask us why we aren't home in bed."

"Why aren't we home in bed?" Chirp muttered, exaggerating a yawn.

"Because we're Indians on a raid, that's why. You think Indians had to worry about curfew?"

Activities in the small Oregon town had ground to a halt except for a cluster of automobiles still parked at Diamond Sally's, where night-owl customers were waiting for Sally and her famous bear to dance their one performance of the evening.

Out of habit Chirp checked for his foster father's new 1940 Chevy, but the coast was clear.

As the boys slipped along in the night shadows of an adjacent factory building, the music from an old Dixieland recording sounded strangely muted and far away, except for sudden moments when the front door of the bar swung open to spit out or swallow a customer and spill a puddle of loud brass and piano notes out into the street.

"Wish it was Satiday," Mugsy said. "Satiday night they got a real live band. That'd be somethin' to hear 'em play 'Muskrat Ramble'!"

Mugsy climbed up on Chirp's shoulders and peered over the wall. "The cage is empty!" Mugsy whispered. "No, wait! There he is! Geez, look at that!"

"Lemme see!" Chirp whispered, buckling under the big boy's weight.

The bear sensed their presence outside the wall, grumbled to his feet, and began to pace the worn concrete floor of his cage. Click, click, click went his long toenails on the rough surface. Standing on his hind legs, the animal seized the heavy iron bars with his great front paws and rattled them as if he meant to loosen them in their sockets. He peered out into the darkness, sniffing the air as though to determine what the intruders were about.

Mugsy crawled up on the wall and pulled Chirp after him. "He's huge!" Chirp gasped. "And look at that big hump on his shoulders. I'm staying right here on the wall. Never knew a bear could be that big!"

The bear dropped to all fours, ambled to the corner of the cage nearest the boys, then rose again to his hind legs and tried to see them better. Standing full height, the bear did look big and menacing. Chirp found himself beset with what-ifs. What if Diamond Sally caught them and held them for their parents? His foster dad had been pretty cranky lately. Worse yet, what if the bear got mad at being touched with a stick and came right through the steel bars of his cage, bending those thick pillars like so many wet noodles? Or what if the giant animal grabbed an arm and pulled the counter of coups right into the cage and ate him? A big boy wouldn't fit through those bars, of course, but that bear was strong enough to make him fit.

Chirp had a sudden desire to be back in his bed. Wild thoughts kept running through his head. He saw Kathryn Anne Weidman's pretty face. She was on the school bus with an empty seat across from her and she kept glancing over, looking sad. As sad as anyone whose best friend had just been eaten by a bear. Chirp realized suddenly that he had forgotten to clean the chicken house before the hens went to roost. The old man had told him to have it done before he went goofing off with that Flanigan kid. Or else! Instead Mugsy had come whistling down the lane, and Chirp had left a note and gone camping.

Mugsy dropped down off the wall into the inner garden, and Chirp was shamed into following. The older boy moved through the shrubbery as if he hadn't a care in the world. He let the branches whip back at Chirp as though it wasn't the function of an Indian chief to care what happened to those behind him.

A branch of coarse, wiry yew wood smacked Chirp right across the face. The boy wiped his dirty cheek with his hand and found blood. BLOOD! What if? What if the giant bear smelled blood and went berserk? A bear's eyesight might be weak but he could sure smell! Chirp remembered reading once that a white boy, camped out somewhere in Montana, had cut his finger on a thorn, and before he could run back to his tent to get a Band-Aid, POW! A bear had him and all they ever found were his suspender buttons and a Boy Scout knife in some bear scat.

Then there was the guy at Chirp's school who swore up and down he had a girl cousin who was camping with her church group in Idaho when a grizzly came in during the night and carried her off, sleeping bag and all. The only traces they ever found were an eight-foot zipper and thirteen hair curlers.

"Hsst! Mugs!" Chirp called, wanting to go home, but the older boy only brandished the coup stick like a sword, flashed him a look of disdain, and moved toward the cage.

Now that they were actually close to the bear, some items came flooding back to Chirp that he had read in the Sunday supplement of the local newspaper about Diamond Sally and her dancing bear. While on her honeymoon in Canada with her fifth husband, Sally bought a cute and cuddly bear cub from an Alberta game farm. She named him "Mr. Beans," thinking he would never get much larger and stay all impish and frolicsome, a pet she could cavort with onstage to distinguish her from other ladies of the dance.

Mr. Beans made his eventual debut on stage and, sure enough, caused an immediate sensation at one of San Francisco's exotic North Beach emporiums. The bear played to a packed house for about a week, when he suddenly seemed to tire of being cute and cuddly.

After climbing the stage curtains, the cub vanished into the upper structures, where he found a napping spot and refused to come down until long after the audience had gone home. That night he shredded the sofa in the apartment in which he,

Sally, and her husband were staying, and the next morning the landlord booted them all out into the street.

Diamond Sally moved to Oregon and used her savings to buy a nightclub, but by the time Mr. Beans was a five-hundred-pound yearling, he was eating zoo rations by the sack and was scarcely to be trusted out of the spacious jail she had constructed for him in the walled-in garden behind the club. Her husband soon tired of cleaning the bear's lair, and departed one morning on a bus headed back to California. He was never seen by Diamond Sally again.

"Beanie, dear," she would say as she fed her pet carefully through the bars, "if only you would be a good little fellow, I could take you on a leash for a walk in the park."

And then she would heave a deep sigh, for, like everyone else around, she knew that Beanie Dear, weighing in at eleven hundred pounds, was getting to the point where he could be dangerous.

Dancing, however, seemed to give the bear a brief respite from boredom and a life of sleeping, eating, and pacing back and forth in his cage. Soon the new concrete showed wear marks where his long toenails clicked at every step and his padded feet scraped upon the damp floor.

Occasionally the public was allowed into the garden, but the bear found no favorites in the crowds that stared at him. Only the rustle of paper from a bag of candy or peanuts could make Mr.

Beans show interest, sit up on his haunches, and beg.

With weak black eyes, he would scan the crowd until he heard paper rustle, then play that person for tidbits by sitting on his haunches, weaving back and forth, catching nuts in mid-throw, or otherwise hamming it up in a half-human manner that brought nervous giggles from the spectators, as though they suspected their own ancestry.

The sudden rattling of a door latch sent both boys scuttling for the bushes. Diamond Sally herself came out into the garden, her fancy costume resplendent even in the faint light of street lamps above the wall. The bear moved expectantly to the cage door and stood waiting, head low, as she slipped a heavy muzzle around his nose and snapped on his collar and lead chain.

"She's beautiful!" Chirp whispered. "Wow! Look at that dress, would you! You suppose it's made of real gold?" He peeked through the shrubbery. "Wish I could see the diamond in her belly button."

"Your taste is all in your mouth," Mugsy whispered. "I think she's ugly. My mother says she makes up for the aging of her body by showing more of it."

The woman opened the cage and led the bear into the nightclub, leaving the door ajar behind her. They heard a burst of applause as Diamond Sally led the bear out onto the stage. Then came the crash of drums and the blat of a trombone as the phonograph launched into a polka.

For a moment the two boys forgot danger as they slipped in through the door and stared in wonder at the scene on the stage. Faster and faster went the music. Faster and faster whirled Diamond Sally. And rearing up on his hind legs, the bear danced round and round beside her, as though aware of the beat.

Chirp could have watched for hours. Enchanted by the flashing lights and the music, he watched open-mouthed until Mugsy suddenly grabbed his arm. The music had stopped.

"Out of here quick! Here they come!"

The boys barely had time enough to hide in the shrubbery before Diamond Sally and Mr. Beans exited the nightclub amidst a roar of applause. Leading the way, the bear seemed to tow her at the end of the leash. "Stop it, you big lunk!" the woman hissed angrily, jerking on the chain.

The bear stopped swiftly in his tracks and swatted at the restraining collar with one huge forepaw. The muzzle, collar, and lead chain clattered to the garden path, and suddenly the bear was free.

The boys clutched each other in terror as the bear rose up on his hind legs to peer about the garden as if he were looking for the intruders. Then, while the woman stood helplessly by, he turned as though habit had won him over and sauntered through the door of his cage.

Three

WHANG! THE GROUND SHOOK as Diamond Sally threw her heavy body at the gate and slammed it shut behind the bear. Click! went the heavy brass padlock on the latch.

"Whew!" the woman muttered, clinging to the bars as though to let her heart start beating again. "Mr. Beans, you did give me a scare!"

The two boys lay behind the prickly yew bushes, trying to become part of the earth. Heart pounding, Chirp clutched his nose, trying to stifle a sneeze. For a moment Diamond Sally seemed to stare in their direction. Then a big gray alley cat darted from the flower garden, leaped a new planting of petunias, and went scratching and clawing over the wall. The neon lights of the nightclub flickered, reflecting off the sequins of Sally's dress, turning the woman on and off like a Christmas tree.

She uncoiled a hose, turned on the water faucet, and sent a gush of water into Mr. Beans' cage, filling his water tank to overflowing, then directed the stream out over the garden to water her plants. For a moment the yew bushes caught the force of the water and left the boys drenched.

"Let's get out of here!" Chirp whispered. "I'm going to charge up over the wall like that old alley cat!" A jet of water arced over the bushes and caught him full in the face, knocking his cap off.

"Wait!" Mugsy hissed. "She'll be done in a minute. Takes more than a little rainstorm to turn back a couple of Indian warriors on a raid."

The wet ground around them began to steam in the warm night air, and Chirp almost choked with the musty smell of decaying leaves and cat urine. The boys lay flat as angleworms on a sidewalk.

"Heck with this! I'm leaving!" Chirp whispered.

"Stay!" Mugsy commanded, as though giving orders to his dog.

Diamond Sally turned off the water, coiled the hose, and took one last look at Mr. Beans. "Go nite-nite now, Mr. Beans. And don't go scaring Mommy like that ever again!"

At the sound of her voice, the bear shuffled over to the door, stood on his hind legs, and rattled the bars of his cage. The woman kissed her fingers, tapped the bear lightly on his forehead through the bars, and went back to her customers.

"Gosh!" Mugsy exclaimed, staggering to his feet. "That was one close call. But that's what makes this whole gig more exciting. I mean, what would an Indian raid be without a little danger?" He glanced at the bear, who peered at them through the bars as though wondering what they were up to at this hour of the night. "It's time," Mugsy said, thrusting the coup stick at Chirp. "Go count coup on that bear!"

Mr. Beans came to their side of the cage and stood tall, gazing down at the boys over his great silvery muzzle as if he were peering over spectacles. Up close the bear was awesome. The Indian boy looked about the garden as though trying to locate a restroom.

"Go ahead!" Mugsy commanded. "Poke him in the chest with that coup stick and let's scram out of here! I dare you!"

"Darers go first!" Chirp replied, his mouth suddenly dry and his voice harsh as a blacksmith's rasp on a summer hoof. "This whole thing was your idea, remember?"

"You're scared!" Mugsy taunted.

"No I ain't, but you are! And you call yourself an Indian chief! I have a notion to call together a tribal council and vote you out. Come to think of it, I'm the whole tribe. This is your last chance to stay chief."

Mugsy glared at Chirp. The bear was standing tall, rubbing one shoulder against the bars as though trying to bend them.

"Go ahead, fraidy cat," Chirp urged. Pushing the coup stick into Mugsy's hands, he shoved the bigger boy forward.

Gritting his teeth, Mugsy stepped over a bed of pansies and sidled toward the animal. The bear moved away from the bars and sat down, panting.

"Go ahead," Chirp urged, secretly thankful to be back where it was safe. "If you're so doggone brave, what are you waiting for?"

The bear glanced at the boys over one shoulder, then seemed to ignore them to stare at the far wall of the cage.

Gingerly Mugsy gripped his coup stick, reached as far as he could into the cage, and poked the animal in the ribs. The bear paid no attention and Mugsy became braver. He swatted the bear across the shoulder.

So swiftly that neither boy saw the animal make his move, the bear slapped the stick away. Feathers humming, the coup stick flew through the air to land with a clatter on the far side of the cage. In a blind panic, Mugsy pulled back his arm, but the bear was faster. He whirled and with both paws raked the boy's arm.

"He got me!" Mugsy screamed, leaping back away from the fence and holding his wounded arm tight against his stomach. "He got me with his claws!"

"Oh, shut up!" Chirping Bird hissed in disgust. "I saw it. Why did you have to hit the bear so hard? So he clawed you a little bit. Think of the fine scars you'll have to show your grandchildren."

White as a snowbank, Mugsy sagged against the wall. "He got me!" he moaned. "Oh, God! I'm bleedin' bad. I'm going to lose this arm! Look!" He pulled up his sleeve. "I can't stand the pain! Quick! Get me a tourniquet! My arm is going to have to come off! I may even die!" A new flood of tears washed down the boy's face, now waxen with shock.

"Aw, come off it," Chirp said. "I've seen more blood out of a squished mosquito. It's not much more than a skin scrape and a long way from your heart. When Mr. Beans batted that stick, you jerked back so fast you probably skinned your arm on the bars." For the first time in their relationship, Chirp was suddenly in control.

"You're a liar!" Mugsy screamed, his hysteria mounting by the moment as shock drove away reason. "He raked me with his claws! Tried to drag me right through the bars. Didn't you see? I want my dad. Where is he? I don't want to die!"

Chirp heard the sound of someone running, and suddenly the courtyard was bathed in light. He had no time to grab Mugsy and hoist him up over the wall.

Dressed in a huge, pink, chenille robe, Diamond Sally came rushing out of the club. "What's happened? What are you boys doing in my garden? What have you done to my poor sweet bear?"

"That bear got me!" Mugsy sobbed, clutching his wounded arm, while a light splattering of blood dropped to the sandy path. "I'm a goner for sure! I was just walking past his cage, minding my own business, when he reached way out and grabbed my arm with his claws. I don't want to die! Get a doctor, ma'am. Oh, hurry! Please!"

No mention was made of the coup stick lying on the floor of the cage, which Mr. Beans was chewing into shreds by now. No mention of the fact that they were trespassing and had climbed a wall to get into the garden.

"It wasn't the bear's fault at all, Miss Sally," Chirp said apologetically. "Mugsy poked his coup stick between the bars and hit the bear a whack on the shoulder. We didn't mean any harm, honest. We were just playing Indians counting coup on the bear."

The woman did not seem to listen. She caught at Mugsy's arm and held the wound toward the light. "Quiet down, kid! It's a nasty scrape, all right, but you'll survive. This is my private property. You had no right to be here."

Mugsy glared at her in defiance. "We heard noises and came over the wall to investigate. We didn't know there was a bear here. Honest!"

The bear stood up next to Diamond Sally and rattled the bars. "Oh, you damned boys! You've upset poor Mr. Beans, and him so tired out after his performance. Quit your caterwauling, boy. Just give me your folks' telephone number and I'll phone and have them meet us in the emergency room at St. Luke's."

Sobbing, Mugsy gave her the number, and she left the boys standing in the garden as she went to call.

"Quick, Mugs, let's get out of here," Chirp cried. "My foster father will kill me if he finds out we got caught in Miss Sally's garden!"

"I can't!" Mugsy sobbed. "I'd never make it over

the wall! I need an ambulance! Why doesn't my daddy come?"

Even at the hospital, Mugsy continued to weep in self-pity. His father rushed down the hospital hall like a raging bull, darting into first one room and then another. He caught a frightened nurse by the collar, demanded his son, then pushed her aside when she was too scared to answer. Chirp heard him coming before he saw him and shook with fear. Mugsy's father was a big man and had been jailed more than once for his foul temper. Suddenly he was upon them and Mugsy was running toward his father, screaming as he went. "Daddy! Daddy! Help me! A grizzly bear tried to eat me!"

When enough hospital attendants had arrived to calm the man down, Chirp built up the courage to speak, to try to tell Mugsy's father what had really happened. "It wasn't the bear's fault, honest, Mr. Flanigan. We were playing Indian, and when Mugsy poked the bear a little hard with his coup stick, the bear clawed at the stick and got Mugsy by mistake!"

Mr. Flanigan stared at Chirp coldly as though wondering how his son happened to be playing with an Indian. "I suppose you're tryin' to tell me that a ninety-pound boy was trying to beat up on a thousand-pound grizzly bear," he snarled.

"It wasn't the bear's fault, Mr. Flanigan, honest!"

Out of control, the big man charged at Chirp, but three husky male attendants grabbed him before he could do Chirp any damage. "You watch your mouth, kid! Nobody's going to call my Algernon a liar!" His face crimson with rage, he strained against the attendants, but they held him fast. "You better hear me," he shouted. "I'm tellin' the whole damn world! Whatever it takes, I'm goin' to see to it that grizzly bear is destroyed!"

Four

THE NEWSPAPERS WERE FULL of it. Mugsy's father saw to that. It wasn't that he was important or had political connections. He had been in and out of jails and asylums because of his violent behavior and people were afraid of him. Some people get more than their share of headlines and Mr. Flanigan was one of them. Chirp dreaded what the headlines would say, but he read them anyway.

Monday's headlines: NIGHTCLUB GRIZZLY MAULS BOY. On Tuesday: MUGSY'S MOTHER FEARS GANGRENE. On Wednesday: CALAMITY FALLS LAD MAY LOSE ARM. By Thursday the newspaper had begun to strain a little more: FLANIGAN TO SUE CITY. Then on Friday came what was to Chirping Bird the most devastating news of all: CITY FATHERS ORDER KILLER BEAR DESTROYED.

Heavily sedated, Mr. Beans was trucked to the

local zoo. On Saturday there was a brief note on page two: ZOO BREAKS ATTENDANCE RECORDS. Everyone was flocking in to see the killer bear, of course, though most folks were disappointed to find that the bear spent most of his time sleeping and during his rare moments of wakefulness, simply paced his new quarters in boredom.

On Sunday, when the crowd was heaviest, a state policeman stopped Mr. Flanigan on his way to the zoo with a loaded big-game rifle. Given the man's reputation for instability, he was arrested for hunting out of season and spent two nights in jail, which only added to his anger. He was released two days later without his rifle, but as he left the station, he screamed back at the desk sergeant that he had plenty more weapons where that came from and he would get revenge on that damn bear yet.

No matter that Chirp gave the police his eyewitness account of what had really happened behind the nightclub that night. No matter that Mugsy's family doctor issued a public report that the bear had done no permanent damage to the boy's arm. No matter that Diamond Sally, dazzling in a new dress purchased for the occasion, pleaded on the steps of City Hall that the life of her old pet be spared. The squeaky wheel gets the grease and Mugsy's father won out. Poor Mr. Beans. Without so much as an official inquiry, the grizzly bear's fate was sealed.

On Tuesday afternoon, Chirp stood in the crowd at the zoo and watched Mr. Beans as he paced back and forth behind the bars of his cage.

"I'm sure glad I'm not that poor bear," he thought. Actually the bear was only one reason for the boy's sadness. Mr. Flanigan had created such a scene down at the waterworks where Chirp's foster father worked that the man lost his job, and his little farm was too small to make a living for his family without that outside work. The old man took it out on Chirp and gave him a good whipping with a willow switch.

"Teach you not to go playing Injun!" he snarled.

Still smarting from that beating, Chirp leaned against the railing in front of Mr. Beans' cage, trying his best to stand in the middle of his trousers so the cloth wouldn't touch his wounds.

He wished he could run away and join Uncle Frank in the Salmon River wilderness in Idaho. Someday, he knew full well, they would be together again.

The big bear came to the front of the cage and sat down to scratch himself. His eyes were deep and dark, but Chirp imagined he saw a sadness there, as though the animal missed his life as a dancing bear.

"Poor Mr. Beans!" Chirp said aloud.

"Poor?" the man next to him snapped. "You're talkin' nonsense, kid. That bear's a killer. He's gotta be put down."

The Indian boy shrugged and moved off a little to where the crowd was thinner, observing suddenly that the bear had followed him to the edge of the cage and was studying him with apparent interest.

"Maybe he can sense who his friends are," Chirp thought. From his pocket he took out a box of Cracker Jack he was hoarding for his supper, tore off one end, poured the sugared peanuts and popcorn into one hand, and tossed them onto the concrete floor of the cage. The big animal shuffled over and cleaned up the feast with his long, pink tongue. Mr. Beans then sat down on his haunches and regarded the boy as though expecting another treat. Chirp couldn't believe his eyes then, for he could have sworn that the big grizzly smiled at him.

Chirp glanced around him at the crowd, but no one seemed to have noticed. The boy fed the rest of the Cracker Jack to the bear and moved back into the silent throng of spectators, aware that the animal had moved to the bars, pulled himself to his full height, and stood looking out as though to see where Chirp was going.

Chirp stopped where the bear could still see him and sat down on a bench. West of the park, he could see the Cascade Mountains where he had spent so much time camping with Uncle Frank. The old man was a Nez Perce from Idaho and had never fit in with the local Klamaths and Modocs. The local authorities claimed he couldn't be a fit parent because he didn't have a job, but it was really reservation politics at work. When it became known that Chirp would be taken away from him and given to foster parents, Uncle Frank left the reservation, brokenhearted, and drifted to Idaho, where his big love was panning for gold and looking for lost mines. Chirp wished desperately that the old man would come back.

"You'd know what to do, Uncle Frank. You wouldn't let them harm that grizzly, would you?"

A light wind caressed the bear's coat like a spring breeze rippling through a ripening field of barley. How many times he'd seen that sight on the reservation when he lived with Uncle Frank. Those were happy times. The old man was always laughing and telling stories. He wore an old baseball cap over his long braided hair, and as he told a tale, he kept grabbing the beak of the cap and worrying it around his head. Sometimes the beak would be facing backwards, sometimes to the side. But always it revolved clockwise. Chirp couldn't ever remember seeing it straight.

When he lived with Uncle Frank they never had much, but they never starved. When he was broke, Uncle Frank would leave him with white neighbors and hitchhike to the Idaho country. Sometimes he would come back with a little sack of gold dust and they would eat well for months. He never talked about where he had his strike, and Chirp never asked. What he did talk about was a cabin he had somewhere in the backcountry of central Idaho, where grizzly bears were his neighbors and the only night lights were the moon and stars.

There in the crowd at the zoo, Chirp could feel the medicine bag beneath his shirt and the pull of its buckskin thong around his neck. He wondered what was in it. An arrowhead for sure; he could feel the shape through the thin leather. Something rattled in there like dried untanned weasel hide. Uncle Frank had given him the bag shortly before they were to be separated.

"Don't open that sack, boy, unless there is a real need," the old man had said.

Chirp thought back on the day Uncle Frank had disappeared. Uncle Frank's team, Buck and Blue, had wandered back across his field with no driver, dragging a spike harrow that left a haphazard road across the newly planted field, then stood waiting patiently at the gate for someone to unhitch them. Some of the neighbors had searched along the nearby lake for his body. But Chirp was sure Uncle Frank wasn't dead. He'd left for Idaho and most likely was afraid someone might follow him to his Idaho gold.

Frank's saddle and saddle horse disappeared with him, and Chirp knew from his stories that he was headed across the Oregon desert, first to Wagontire, then Burns, then over Stinkingwater Pass to Idaho. Down deep Chirp felt that someday Uncle Frank would send for him. The neighbor, Charley Redfox, had dropped by conveniently that morning to borrow an ax and stayed on until the boy's new foster parents picked him up. It was obvious to Chirp that Redfox knew more than he was telling; Uncle Frank had engineered his showing up at the farm. Redfox was too old to thirst for gold. Even with the old neighbor's presence, however, Chirp remembered feeling helpless, as helpless as that dancing bear.

It was getting toward closing time at the zoo now, and the crowd was thinning fast, leaving a mess of candy wrappers, cigarette butts, and spilled popcorn where it had stood to view the renegade bear. A couple of overweight ravens were waddling back and forth, guarding the booty from some seagulls and blackbirds.

Mr. Beans sat looking out at the humans as though waiting for one last batch of peanuts. His front paws were folded across his tummy. He didn't look mean, just big. His head was broad and his dark eyes, tinted with cinnamon, were expressionless. No telling what the animal was really thinking. Maybe how nice it would be to be out of there, wandering in a cool green forest, where there were lots of ripe berries, the streams were full of fish, and the logs packed with delicious juicy boreworm grubs.

Chirp looked up to see two policemen approaching. They stood for a moment, looking at the bear, then one of them checked his watch.

"It's 4:30!" he said. "An hour till closing. When the crowd's gone, we'll get the rifles from the squad car and fix that bear so he'll never hurt another kid."

The policemen suddenly noticed Chirp sitting in the shade and stopped talking.

The boy looked quickly at the bear as though he feared the animal might have understood. Mr. Beans seemed to be busy watching a big bluebottle fly, which buzzed his nose as though it knew better than to land. Then the bear got up off his haunches and began to pace the floor, toenails clicking monotonously on concrete.

"They can't kill Mr. Beans!" the boy muttered to himself. "It's all like a bad dream. That bear didn't do anything to deserve dying. Why won't people believe me?"

He sensed that the real trouble lay with Mugsy's dad, Mr. Flanigan. People were afraid to cross him. He'd stood trial for wife-beating and assault, but all the courts ever did was send him off for treatment, and he seemed to come back more resentful than before. Chirp couldn't understand how Mugsy could like his father. Maybe, deep down, he was scared of what life might be like if, like Chirp, he had no parents at all.

Chirp looked at his watch. Forty-five minutes left. He had to do something fast. He slipped out of the thinning crowd, put a building between himself and the two policemen, and started to run.

As he rushed out the zoo gate, he almost crashed into Mr. Flanigan, who could be expected to show up at 5:30 to make sure the police did their duty. The man shot him a look of hatred and picked up a rock as though to fling it at him. He seemed to blame Chirp for what had been Mugsy's idea to count coup on the bear.

Chirp's foster father was sitting on the front porch drinking beer. He glowered at the boy as though he were angry at him for running, for using all that energy playing instead of working. Chirp plowed on past him before the man could gather his wits to speak.

In the garage he found the old man's toolbox and took out a hacksaw and three blades. Moments later he was off and running, using the creek bed as cover. As he scampered away, he heard the man shouting his name, but he only hurried faster.

The zoo gates slammed shut just as he came puffing up. "We're closing early today!" the ticket taker said. "You can't go in!" He seemed to be eyeing the bulge in the boy's shirt, where Chirp had hidden the hacksaw.

"I left my jacket in there!" Chirp said. "I laid it down right by the pelican display, and if I've lost it my old man will murder me!"

"Well, okay," the man said, opening the gate a little. "But move your bones, boy. There's a ball game on tonight!"

The two policemen were sitting in their squad car and Mr. Flanigan was talking to them through the window. Using a hedge of Russian olive trees as a screen, Chirp cut down an alley behind the cages. A captive red fox yapped at him, and a pair of coyotes started a chorus. At the rear of the bear house was a big iron door of half-inch plate. Windowless and forbidding, it was fastened with a rusty iron chain big enough to tow a locomotive and locked with a heavy brass padlock.

Chirp took the hacksaw, put on a new blade, and began sawing. The first blade broke on the hard steel of the lock and clattered to the ground.

He put on a new blade and tried sawing the chain instead. It was softer metal, but he was in too much of a hurry and the second blade broke in two.

One blade left! He slowed down and worked with long, even, one-directional strokes. He could hear the big animal on the other side, sniffing at the crack under the door, trying to get his scent.

He heard car doors slam as the policemen got out of their vehicle and headed toward the bear cage. "I can't do it!" Chirp whispered in anguish. "I've still got some to go!"

He made one last attempt with the saw, then gave the chain a jerk. The rusty link crumbled and fell to the concrete. It clattered loudly and Chirp hoped the police hadn't heard.

Grasping the big iron door with both hands, he swung it open and stood face-to-face with the big bear.

"C'mon, Mr. Beans! Run for it! They're planning to shoot you!" Chirp pleaded with the bear as he backed away.

The bear stepped out on the concrete apron behind his pen and sniffed for a moment as though analyzing the boy's tracks, then suddenly seemed to realize that he was free. He leaped off the concrete and went lumbering across the meadow.

"Run! Oh, run, Mr. Beans! Get out of here before they shoot!" Chirp ran for the forest, hoping the bear would follow.

At the edge of the forest, Chirp turned and, from his vantage point, saw Mr. Flanigan and the two policemen moving quickly around the corner of the bear cage toward the alley.

Mr. Beans struck a patch of green grass and stopped to graze. He stood now in the middle of a large clearing, in full view of his enemies. There was a sudden shout from one of the policemen, who had spotted the bear and raised his rifle. The rifle jerked in the man's hands, a gout of gravel spouted under the bear, and a loud bang echoed along the edge of the forest.

The bear leaped into the air as though stung. At last some long-dormant instinct for survival triggered his fear, and the bear ran for the woods.

Another burst of rifle fire staggered the bear and he went down, biting angrily at his shoulder. Then, suddenly, the animal was up again, galloping pell-mell for a patch of wild plum bushes. Moments later Chirp saw Mr. Beans charge through the chain-link fence surrounding the grounds, flattening it as though it were made of cardboard. Using a windfall as a screen, the bear vanished into the forest. For the first time in his life, Mr. Beans was free!

Five

SIRENS STIRRED THE TOWN and sent the zoo coyotes into a hysteria of howls. Within minutes, however, the streets of Calamity Falls emptied and became silent as death as word that the killer bear was wounded and loose on the town spread over radio, telephones, and backyard fences. Folks grabbed their young ones and barred their doors, expecting any moment to hear scratchings from without.

Joe Esher closed down his service station and went home to his wife. "I've been keeping score," Joe told the woman. "I've already heard about fifteen people that were mauled by that bear and eaten. Way I see it, if that animal were wounded, he'd just head for the woods, find some place to lick his wounds and hide. Why that bear wouldn't hurt a doggone flea. There ain't a man in town hasn't fed him peanuts at Diamond Sally's. Just to be safe though, better help me unplug the 'frigerator and shove it in front of the door."

His wife eyed him curiously as they slid the refrigerator across the floor. "Sounds like you've been to Diamond Sally's lots of times to know the bear that well."

Down at the town square, the police were begging for volunteers, handing out rifles to experienced hunters who might want to go hunt bear. Pickup loads of Indians off the reservation drove into town, the back windows of their trucks loaded with rifles. Spotlights for night hunting were mounted like third eyes above the cabs.

Sergeant Wimer thought a minute before handing Mr. Flanigan a rifle, but this was an emergency. "You behave yourself, Flanigan, you hear? Just don't go shootin' to be shootin'. There's going to be a lot of hunters in our skirmish line, and I don't want anyone shot."

Mr. Flanigan took the rifle and grabbed a box of ammunition from the trunk of a police car but said nothing. Already his mind seemed far away in pursuit of the bear. His eyes were as flat as two pennies. Black, unemotional. For a moment, the policeman wished he had not issued the man a rifle, but it was too late. He knew he wouldn't get the rifle back without an argument.

"John," Sergeant Wimer said to his partner, "you patrol the town. I don't want people out of their houses until we've got the bear. The rest of us will take off trackin' blood. As bad as he must be bleedin' from that shoulder, it should be an easy track to follow."

Sergeant Wimer looked about him at the ragtag army of volunteers assembling on the zoo lawn and wondered how many of them had ever shot guns before. Otis, the town handyman, had a club-foot, but Wimer knew he would be as steady in an emergency as anyone. Except for the Indians, who hunted for sustenance, the rest would do as brush beaters and little more.

"Let's go, men!" the sergeant said. "Otis and I will take the trail, and the rest of you wing out in a skirmish line about thirty feet from each other. I don't want any talkin', and be careful. I don't want any of you brought back in a body bag." He looked around for Mr. Flanigan and swore under his breath. He was gone! That creep! He had slipped away and was following the blood trail alone!

Six

CHIRP FOUND A SPATTER OF FRESH BLOOD where Mr. Beans had passed over the weathered gray of a fallen pine. He covered the red medallion with dead pine needles and rushed on, following what tracks he could find. The bear seemed intent upon leaving civilization behind and was heading straight for the dark forests of the Cascade Mountains, just three miles away.

The boy realized that turning the bear loose hadn't been the smartest thing to do, but he had been given little choice. And the policeman? Taking a long shot that chanced wounding the bear and turning him into a vicious killer hadn't been the smartest thing either.

A hungry grizzly loose in a rural area was bad enough, but a wounded, angry animal with no fear of man might be capable of exploding into a death charge at the first sight of a human. Up ahead Chirp saw thickets of young yellow pine growing close as hair on a dog. The boy sensed that entering this gloomy labyrinth to follow the bear's trail was foolhardy, but he felt a responsibility now to keep track of Mr. Beans and maybe prevent some innocent people from getting hurt.

If only the bear would skirt the populated areas until he gained the thick rocky forests where there were few settlements! Aware that a posse of trackers was on their trail, the boy erased any flecks of blood or bear tracks as he went.

Now and again he caught sight of the big animal in the distance and rushed forward, gaining an advantage on the pursuers as he ran, for they would have to earn every inch of that distance by slow, laborious tracking.

As he came to the edge of a draw, he saw the huge bear standing in the shadows, his good paw braced against a rock, looking back on his tracks. "Please, Mr. Beans!" he called out. "Run for it! Head for the mountains! I'll follow along behind."

The bear stood on both hind legs to get a better look, then turned, slowly and stiffly, and moved off into the scrub. The animal was limping painfully, packing one front leg, but still the pace made Chirp puff to keep up.

He felt a strange camaraderie with Mr. Beans. By now folks would have discovered that the chain on the cage had been cut and found the hacksaw lying in the dirt where he had dropped it as he ran. It wouldn't be hard to identify him as the culprit. The gatekeeper would give the police a good description. They would be hunting him now as well as the bear; he and Mr. Beans were in this thing together.

As they headed west, the scrub oak and pine opened up a bit, although the land was still steep and rugged. The bear's trail crossed a shallow mountain stream, and Chirp fancied that the animal had stopped to drink. But he found splash marks where the bear had plunged on through and up the far bank. Breaking off a fir branch, Chirp brushed out the tracks as best he could and continued on.

West of the stream, the tracks were increasingly hard to follow. As he gained the top of a ridge, the boy saw the shining summer snowfields of the Cascades gleaming in the distance. He found where the bear had paused to bed down for a few moments on a patch of tan pine needles. Chirp was relieved that there were only a few scattered drops of blood.

Some instinct seemed to be leading Mr. Beans toward the mountains, skirting civilization, but suddenly, just as Chirp thought he had the bear figured out, a dozen mule deer jumped from their beds ahead of him. The bear shied away and headed back down the timbered hillsides to where the spire of a country church gleamed white against the dark of the pines.

The boy groaned aloud. There were a few lonely,

scattered farms down there where children might be playing unaware of danger. A wild bear would probably keep to himself, but a wounded animal packing a grudge and with no fear of people could be a disaster. He had to get closer to the bear so that he might warn people of the danger!

Outside the church, he saw a delivery truck and guessed that it was old Mr. Gustavson delivering a load of communion wine. Suddenly Chirp caught sight of the giant grizzly. He was standing at the edge of the church shrubbery, sniffing the air as though for food.

Intent on warning Mr. Gustavson, Chirp circled through the trees and climbed the picket fence into the church yard, but by the time he caught sight of Mr. Beans, the bear's fat behind was just disappearing into the back of the delivery van.

The truck lurched and canted sideways as if it were going to tip over, then righted itself. Boxes of groceries and jugs erupted through the door; glass shattered and wine flowed like blood from door to pavement as though the van were bleeding to death. Mr. Beans came out of the truck with a large ham in his mouth, sat down in a puddle of wine, and made short work of the meat. Then, discovering the sweet, fruity liquor purpling the gutter beside him, the feverish animal began to drink.

Suddenly there was the old groceryman whistling down the sidewalk, swinging his truck keys on a thong. He was almost to the vehicle when he noticed the carnage.

"Run, Mr. Gustavson!" Chirp shouted as the bear stood on his hind legs to get a good look at the human.

The old man did not need to be warned. He sprinted for his truck, leaped in, slammed the door, started the engine, backed into the bear, knocking him aside, and roared up the hill. A lone watermelon shot from the truck like a peace offering for the bear, then rolled back down the slope to shatter against a curb.

In the distance, against the roar of the departing truck, Chirp could hear sirens, but it was hard to separate the sounds from the echoes. One thing he knew! Within minutes the police would be surrounding them, and he feared that Mr. Beans would be sitting on the ground drunk in full view of everyone. There would be more rifles now, at closer range, and he doubted that many of the bullets would miss.

"You dumb old bear!" Chirp shouted angrily, waving his fist at the animal.

For a few moments, the bear lapped wine, then, his thirst quenched, he rose unsteadily, looked off in the direction of the sirens, belched a great belch, and staggered back in the direction of the forest.

"Let that drunken old bear take care of himself!" Chirp muttered angrily. "I'm through with him! Soon the woods will be swarming with deputies and I got my own neck to think about!" He turned and ran through the pines until his sides ached and his breath came in gasps. He paused only to look for glimpses of snowy peaks through the trees to make sure he was heading west.

In the distance he heard a new sound, the baying of hounds. Dogs following a blood trail would find Mr. Beans in short order. There wasn't much chance for the big bear now. Pausing to look back on his trail, he caught sight of the poor animal. The wine had worked on the grizzly. Crossing a fallen log on three legs, the huge bear slipped and crashed down on his chest; he seemed ready to lie there forever.

"Get up, Mr. Beans!" Chirp screamed, starting back down the hill toward the animal. The bear seemed to hear him and staggered to his feet, sniffing the ground as he moved forward as though trying to pick up the boy's trail.

He saw the bear fall over another log and lie for what seemed an eternity, then struggle back to his feet and slide down a sandy slope into a stream.

Chirping Bird was running with long leaps down the hillside to help the bear when he saw a posse of men in the distance converging on the point where he had last seen Mr. Beans. There were sudden shouts as the men sighted their quarry; a fusillade of shots echoed back and forth across the canyon. "Poor Mr. Beans," the boy thought. "That's got to be the end of him now!"

Moving into a thicket of mountain mahogany, Chirp used it as cover to get as far from the scene as possible. Slipping across a saddle between two bare lava humps, he paused to get his bearings. Down in the canyon where he had last seen Mr.

Beans, the stream showed golden in the dying sun, but the boy fancied that the water gleamed with a touch of rose, as though stained with Mr. Beans' blood.

He heard hounds baying again, and spotted them milling up and down the edge of the stream where the bear had slid into the water. Why, after that barrage of rifle fire, were they still looking for the bear?

Chirp dropped suddenly to the ground and lay behind a log. Four men were almost upon him. Three were uniformed state troopers and the fourth was his foster father, looking gray and grim, helping them track him down.

They passed silently just on the other side of the log, and once they were headed down one ridge, he plunged down another into the gathering dusk. He had one intention now, to put as many miles as possible between himself and civilization. He would rather live the life of a wild Indian in the mountains than be captured and sent back to captivity.

He was getting hungry. Looking about him in the dusk, he wondered what his ancestors would have done about food. Mugsy had read a lot of books about Indians; maybe he would have known what to eat. But Mugsy had failed him and now seemed lost to him forever.

Chirp found some watercress in a small seep spring. On the other side of the water, a pine squirrel, daring owls and other night hunters, sat on an old rotten log and scolded him, then scampered into a hole for the night. The boy tore the log apart with his hands, found the squirrel's cache of pine seeds, rubbed a handful between his palms to de-wing them, then wolfed them down, hulls and all. They tasted so good, he stayed there until he could no longer see what he was eating. After filling his pockets with seed from the log and watercress from the spring, he drank deeply of the sweet water and moved once more toward the mountains, traveling slowly, carefully, as his eyes adjusted to the darkness.

As night fell, the cool moist air descended the slope to fill the hollows and Chirp could feel it on his hot face. There was a time of near total darkness when he had to grope his way, stumbling over logs and tearing his clothes on branches, but soon a bright moon appeared over the eastern ridges and he could travel with ease once more. As it rose higher, the moon got smaller and smaller and soon was a hard yellow lantern above his head, guiding him on his way.

Once he stopped and listened carefully. He thought he could hear dead limbs snapping in the distance as though something big were following his trail, but when he huddled for a time to catch his breath, there was only silence.

Ahead of him in the moonlight loomed a long rimrock of volcanic lava. He climbed carefully over a field of shattered rock to the base of the cliff, then searched for a way up and over the natural barrier. What fissures he found and tried to climb always ended abruptly just as he thought he had reached the top. He was close to exhaustion when he came to the dark entrance of a cave in the rocks.

Standing at the entrance, he wondered whether or not he dared enter. There was the rank smell of mountain lions in the air, and he hoped that they merely used the cave in passing and were not lurking inside waiting for him to sacrifice himself. The chill wind off the mountain snowfields started the pine boughs above his head to soughing mournfully. Shivering, he moved cautiously into the cave, exploring as far back as the dim light of the moon permitted.

There was a mustiness about the cave; many a cougar, pack rat, marmot, or porcupine had owned it before him. A pack rat scampered along a ledge and disappeared into a mound of sticks and rubble. Somehow Chirp felt glad for its company.

He wished he'd brought some matches for a fire, but he searched his pockets and found nothing but an old pocketknife whose blades were rusty and broken. He tried to make a fire by rubbing two sticks together, but grew exhausted by the effort and produced not even the smell of smoke. Far off in the V between two hills, he could see the night lights of Calamity Falls.

There would be lots of excitement as the hunters returned from the hills. If the bear still lived, the streets would be deserted as though folks expected it to raid the town. If the bear were dead, of course, the men would be heroes.

In his mind Chirp heard again that dreadful volley of shots. No animal could have survived that hail of bullets. Most likely there would be dancing on Main Street now, and the taverns would be loud with stories and exaggeration. Still, the boy remembered, the hounds had been uncertain. There was the off chance that it had been just dark enough for the bear to escape.

Lying in the soft dirt against one wall of the cave, he pillowed his cheek against his arm and soon passed into an exhausted sleep, but some hours later, he awoke to night noises. Someone or something was creeping up the talus slope toward him.

The moon had passed above the rimrock and no longer bathed the entrance of the cave in light. He raised himself on one elbow and listened. High in the rocky ceiling, bats squeaked from crevasses in the roof. Down the hillside on the talus slope, a rock was dislodged, slid, rattled, then fell for what seemed an eternity before landing with a muffled thump below.

Seven

THE CAVE THAT HAD SHELTERED HIM suddenly felt like a prison. In the gloom he tried to make out the shape of the walls, hoping there was another exit, or at least a crack he could wedge himself into and hide, but he could see nothing. He considered rushing out the cave entrance and fleeing up over the rimrock above, charging across that rocky devil's garden of a landscape to escape. Or should he lie still on the off chance that whoever or whatever was out there would fail to find the mouth of the cave and go away?

He flattened himself against the rough, damp wall as though to seem part of it, hardly daring to breathe. In the darkness his hand closed on a small rock the size of a baseball, but he realized that as a weapon the rock was like a grain of sand in the face of his danger.

From somewhere deeper in the cave, he heard frightened squeaks and scramblings, as though mice had sensed the evil and were desperate to claw their way out. High on the ceiling, bats began to rustle restlessly, chittering their high-pitched unoiled sonar, then began to desert their roosts and pour out the entrance of the cave.

Chirp could see a faint twinkling of far-off city lights, then, suddenly, the lights were blotted out as a huge body blocked the door, and the cave was plunged into total darkness. From the heavy smell of bear and booze, Chirp realized that the bear had been following his trail and had finally caught up to him. Just what he could expect now, he didn't know.

The bear groaned with pain as he squeezed past the rocks. For a moment he seemed to be stuck in the hole, then, as suddenly as they had vanished, the distant lights of the town came back. Chirp heard the click of toenails on rock as the animal padded about, investigating the cave. Once the bear stumbled as though he was still feeling the effects of all that wine. Chirp heard the bear sniff the air to locate his hiding place, and he tensed, expecting at any moment to feel those great claws tearing at his body and those yellowed teeth cracking the bones of his legs as easily as they had demolished the coup stick.

But there was only a loud groan as the bear sank suddenly to the sand. Soon Chirp heard the sound of the bear's rough tongue licking his shoulder. Chirp's heart beat loud in his chest.

56

The boy lay still against the rocks. He felt a heavy, cold-footed spider walk across his cheek. The spider seemed to be spinning a web from his face to the wall. He hoped it wasn't a black widow, or, worse yet, a brown recluse. He wanted desperately to brush the spider away, but he dared not move.

Long minutes passed. The bear ceased to lick. His head was up now and he panted with exertion. Through the door of the cave, the town lights were dimming as more and more households went to sleep. Chirp could see a few stars in the northern heavens and wished he could float outward into space and land on a star where there were no Mr. Flanigans, and no men with guns.

From time to time, Chirp's eyelids grew heavy and his mind wandered with fatigue, but he could not sleep. His muscles ached from all that running and climbing. The spider finished its web, chaining the boy to the rocks. In the blackness near his ear, he heard a sudden fluttering as a night moth got caught in the web and struggled to free itself. Then all sounds ceased.

In spite of his fears, Chirp drifted off, and when he opened his eyes again, the stars had faded and there was a faint hint of rose in the sky. Judging by the sounds, the bats were back in the cave. Despite the terrors of the night, he was still alive. In the gloom he could make out the outline of the sleeping bear.

Mr. Beans was lying in the center of the cave,

his head turned slightly away. A faint glimmering of hope came to the boy. Maybe he could sprint for the mouth of the cave and dive through before the bear could fully awake. Chirp moved slightly, breaking the spiderweb. A pair of moth wings fluttered to the floor, and a big brown spider hurried toward a crack in the rocks.

He could see the bear's wound, a patch of crimson where the bullet had struck the shoulder bone. Already the edges of the bullet hole had turned black. Grass and pine needles, congealed in blood, clung to his hide.

The shoulder was swollen and the animal clearly had lost agility, but how much? What were Chirp's chances of getting out that door?

Slowly, without taking his eyes off the bear, Chirp raised himself on one elbow. The grizzly sensed the movement and turned his massive head to watch, but made no other move.

"Take it easy, Mr. Beans. I'm not the one that hurt you. I just want out of the mess we're in. Just lie there quietly, big bear, and let me make it out that entrance and you can have this cave for your very own. I won't bother you again. No sirree! Honest Injun!"

Slowly, carefully, Chirp got to his knees, leaning against the rocks as blood began to circulate through his cramped limbs. He inched forward along the wall, keeping as far away from the bear as possible.

Mr. Beans seemed to sense his intentions and

lumbered to his feet, blocking the boy's escape. But he meant Chirp no harm.

"Look at him!" Chirp said. "I think he's afraid I'll leave him behind. Miss Sally raised him from a cub and she was all the life he had. Now she's gone and he's lost in a world of hurt. Maybe that's why he followed my trail, as though he wanted me to take her place and take care of him." A moment ago Chirp's thought had been to escape the bear. Now he knew it was up to him to help the bear escape.

The boy sat down and leaned against the wall, his head in his hands. "Why me, Mr. Beans?" he asked. "I don't know how to save myself, let alone you. I know you didn't mean me any harm, but you must have left a trail up the ridge even an idiot could follow. I don't know how you managed to give those hounds a slip down by the stream, but today's a whole new chance for the hunters to find your trail. And thanks to you, that trail will lead right up the hill to this cave."

The bear lay back and resumed licking his wounds. The animal's nose was dry with fever and he did not seem much interested in the world around him. Chirp set about digging out rocks that had fallen from the ceiling over the years and rolled them to the entrance. He placed them carefully, blocking the entrance so only the bats could fly through. Now, at least, the bear could not go wandering out at the wrong moment and be spotted by hunters, yet Chirp himself could crawl out simply by rolling one of the rocks out of the way.

He left the cave for a cautious look around. Above him towered the great, gray rimrock, which marked a flow of ancient lava. It stretched north and south like a huge scar. Here and there the rim was cracked with fissures, but none a wounded bear could climb. To escape the area, one would have to slip past either end of the rimrock through thickets of mountain mahogany and stunted pine. There would be deer trails there, but Chirp assumed that a bear hunter would be stationed on every trail. Their only chance was to hide in the cave until the hunters gave up and went back to town. The cave seemed to be hidden well enough by thickets, but Chirp scattered a few pine needles over the rocks, then brushed out what tracks he could find. For a time the boy stood listening, thankful that he could not hear the baying of hounds, then crawled back in and sealed the entrance until only a small window of light showed whether it was day or night. To anyone passing by, the cave would seem to be only a roosting place for bats.

Eight

WHAT CHIRP COULD NOT HAVE KNOWN was that Mr. Beans had already met the enemy on the field of battle and won a victory of sorts. The hounds had caught up with the wounded bear and cornered him against the thrust-up roots of a giant Douglas fir windfall. With his one good paw, Mr. Beans sent one overzealous hound to his reward. Two other dogs were accounted for by hunters who ignored the safety of the dogs to fire a volley at the bear. As so often happens when a hunter's quarry is at close range, the men fired without aiming, and killed the dogs. Then the bear slipped around the windfall and disappeared in the gathering dusk.

Chirp had heard the volley and decided prematurely that the hunters had scored. By the time the bear picked up Chirp's trail and followed him up the hill to the cave, the angry and disgusted dog handler had loaded his diminished pack into a deputy sheriff's truck and was headed back to his kennels.

Now with the morning sun filtering into the cave, Chirp sat and regarded his friend. He reached into his jacket pocket, scraped up his last remaining handful of pine nuts, and set them on a rock for the bear. Mr. Beans gazed at the offering with sunken eyes, sniffed the pile but rejected it. Tucking his head between his paws, he went back to sleep. Chirp realized that he had one sick bear on his hands; there was a sadness to the animal that even hinted at death.

Chirp slipped past the bear and took his place by the wall. The cave spider had begun a new web but seemed to think better of the location and climbed back up to the rocky ceiling.

"Please get better, Mr. Beans," the boy whispered. "You've just got to."

The animal lifted his head, aiming the stubby cones of his ears at the boy as though to catch every word. Once more the animal began licking his wound, but the effort seemed to tire him and he closed his eyes.

In the distance Chirp heard a new sound, the throb of a light airplane patrolling the forest. He peered from the blocked-in entrance but his field of vision was too narrow. Then for a moment he caught sight of the airplane so far down the mountain he could see sunlight shining on the top of its wing. It was a small Piper Cub, the kind used by fire patrols over at the Indian agency.

The craft explored the hillside, flying low, patrolling back and forth like a giant dragonfly. For a few minutes, the pilot made repeated runs over a heavy patch of downed timber as though to spook the bear out of it. So slowly Chirp feared that the plane would fall out of the air, the pilot traversed the long rimrock as if to convince himself that the bear could not have found a way up over the rim.

As the airplane flew low over the mouth of the cave, the roar was deafening, but the bear was lost in sleep and never moved. Soon, to Chirp's relief, the plane moved off and began a systematic search of the thickets west of the cave.

Far down the hillsides, Chirp heard men shouting as they circled, trying to detect bear tracks where they had last seen the animal, but the trail was getting cold and the land was probably so disturbed by human footprints that tracking would soon be impossible.

For a time the boy gave in to exhaustion and dozed, despite every effort to stay awake. He awoke to new sounds. Someone was on the rimrock above the cave, throwing rocks off the rim as though trying to flush the bear from heavy cover.

One of the rocks thudded to the earth right in front of the entrance to the cave. A chipmunk scampered to safety and began scolding from a rotten log. Another rock crashed to the right of the entrance, and a rock wren piped and flew low down the rocky slope to a safer bit of cover.

There was silence for a time. When Chirp dared

move a rock and peer up at the rimrock, the man was visible around a bend, but he was on the move, holding his rifle with his left hand and hurling rocks down the hill with his right. Then, suddenly, he was lost from view. For some time the boy sat watching, but the man did not reappear.

Chirp's mouth felt as if it were filled with cotton and his stomach hurt with hunger. A few hundred feet away, there was a seep spring. Despite his narrow field of vision, he could see a doe working her way up the hill to drink, and judging from the time she spent drinking, he knew there had to be at least some suckable water there. The boy reasoned that it was wiser to wait until dusk before leaving the cave, but his thirst was urgent. He waited until the deer had passed on down the hill, then slid a rock out of the entrance and crawled out the hole. Hugging the rim, he found a crevasse leading up the rocks, climbed the rough, lichened surfaces, and peered over the edge. As far as he could see in both directions, the coast was clear.

He climbed back down and crept to the spring, swept away a host of drinking hornets with his hat, and sucked up mouthfuls of pure sweet water, ignoring the whirlybugs and water striders that danced away from his nose. Before he left to return to the cave, he filled his hat for the bear.

There was only half a hatful left when he crawled back into the cave. He set the water down where the bear could reach it, then retreated.

The bear lifted his head groggily, sniffed the

water, slurped it up, and looked for more. Chirp reached out with a stick to retrieve his hat and made another stealthy trip to the spring.

Shouting again. The enemy was covering a ridge to the west. Perhaps the bear had made a sashay across it, then doubled back, looking for Chirp's trail. The trail was confusing the hunters. A smarter tracker would have cut larger and larger circles and found where the bear had left the area of the last good track.

The spring seemed to gather a little volume as it moved downhill. Where the current was swifter, the spring was choked with watercress. The boy pulled up greens by the handful, washed out mud from the roots and bugs from the leaves, then wolfed down the tangy, succulent greens, suspecting that maybe he was getting more water than food value. But he felt better with something, at least, in his stomach.

For half an hour, he sat hidden in the thickets beside the spring, analyzing every sound that came to him. High in the ponderosa pines, a pair of Clarke's nutcrackers were as noisy as crows. Western tanagers flashed orange and yellow as they fed in the chokecherry bushes. From higher on the ridges, a fox sparrow poured out its soul in song. Chirp wondered how there could be danger in such a peaceful world. Feeling safe for the moment, he carried a great dripping armload of watercress to the bear.

Suspicious at first, the bear began licking up the

greens, but soon tired and went back to sleep. Chirp crept softly past the animal and out the entrance, replacing the rocks carefully as he left. A half mile from the cave, Chirp found a place where a logger had dumped the garbage from a logging camp over the rim. Scavenging, he found two gallon tomato cans that were not yet rusted through, plus a length of wire. Fitting the cans with wire bails, he made a pair of buckets he could use for gathering, cooking, and packing water to the bear.

The woods were still dangerous, but pausing for long periods to make sure no one was around, he brought bucket after bucket of water to Mr. Beans and watched with satisfaction as the bear lapped it up. He looked for a change in the bear, but the animal's nose was still cracked and dry, and his eyes still showed his distress.

"You'll get better, Mr. Beans!" the boy said aloud, as though hoping his saying it would make it come true.

Chirp remembered back on the farm when Uncle Frank's favorite draft horse had fallen in the cattle guard and lost some hide, and the old Indian gathered a bucket of pine pitch, melted it over a fire, and applied that to the wound. Maybe it was the pitch or the fact that Uncle Frank sat up every night chanting and pounding on his drum, but the miracle happened and the horse got so well you had to look hard to find a scar.

Chirp felt he owed it to Mr. Beans to give it a try. From the bark of a lightning-scarred ponderosa he scraped bullets of amber pitch until his bucket was almost full, then set about building a fire in the cave.

He had already failed at making a fire by rubbing two sticks together. Now he took a leather lace from one of his boots and made a toy bow out of supple green willow, then found a straight stick for a drill shaft. It was just what Uncle Frank had done once when he had forgotten matches to light his pipe.

Taking a handful of dried grass and some tinder-dry duff from the heart of a rotten pine, Chirp looped the bowstring around the drill shaft, placed the point in the rotten wood, and began to saw back and forth with the bow. To the boy's relief, the point of the shaft whirled back and forth like a drill in the duff and grew hot from friction. A wisp of smoke arose, a ruby coal glowed, went out, and glowed again, and soon, Chirp was able to blow the coal into a flame.

He melted the pitch in the bucket over the fire until it flowed like honey. When it was cool, he dipped in a long stick and smeared the pitch on the bear's wound.

Mr. Beans came awake with a start, knocking the stick away with one swipe of his paw. Patiently Chirp picked up the stick, let the bear sniff it, then dipped it once more in the bucket. The animal seemed to grasp that the boy was trying to help and lay back with a sigh. Soon the whole angry wound was covered with a heavy yellow crust of pine pitch.

Once his doctor work was done, the boy slipped out of the cave to scavenge for food. He found another pine squirrel cache in a rotten log, stole a meal of pine seeds, then took a sharp stick and dug up roots in the rocky lava soil above the rim. At dusk he dared to venture out on the open flats where he dug for the roots of the white-panicled flower Uncle Frank had called "ipos." The digging was hard, but each plant yielded a cluster of rootlets resembling olive pits, which, eaten raw, tasted like a cross between a peanut and a potato.

Chirp packed his buckets back to the cave, mashed the rootlets with a flat stone, then kneaded the dough into cakes, which he baked before a small fire. He thought to offer some to the bear, but the animal was burning up with fever. He lay with his muzzle tucked under his chest, his forehead flat upon the ground.

To a hungry boy, the cakes tasted delicious. He paced the cave, anxious to use the cover of darkness to be gone, to put some distance between themselves and civilization. But he could not leave Mr. Beans sick and helpless, surrounded by human enemies.

It was a week before the fever broke, and by then, the hunt for the grizzly seemed to have died down. Perhaps folks assumed that the bear had died of its wounds by now. In his endless search for food, Chirp was able to venture far from the cave, scouting out escape routes he could take once the bear was able to travel.

Under its great crust of pine pitch, the bear's wound did seem to be healing, and his eyes no longer were sunken with fever. One morning, when Chirp came to the entrance of the cave, the bear sat up on his haunches and begged, just as he had done for peanuts in the zoo.

Despite the time he had spent as Mr. Beans' companion, Chirp carried memories of how the animal had knocked the coup stick out of Mugsy's hand. The boy still kept a certain distance, particularly when food was involved. He had a real respect for the bear's savage strength and explosive temper.

One night, as Chirp awoke from an exhausted sleep, he found that the big grizzly had moved during the night and now lay with his muzzle against the boy's knee. Chirp felt his heart hammering, then overcame his fear to reach out and scratch the inner cone of those short, stubby ears. Mr. Beans merely opened one eye and closed it again. But he tilted his head submissively for more grooming.

The chill of early morning had crept into the cave and Chirp snuggled closer to the bear for warmth. For a time he lay absorbing the heat of the great animal against his back, feeling safe for the moment from the bear's anger. Then he thought once more of the danger they both were in. They were still too close to civilization, and sooner or later, someone would encounter him on his foraging expeditions and report him. The hunt would be on again with renewed vigor.

As he sat before a tiny fire, the boy fingered his

medicine bag. Uncle Frank had warned him not to open the sack except in an emergency. Chirp wondered if there ever could be a greater emergency than this.

With the stubby blade of his pocketknife, Chirp cut the sinew holding the sack shut and drew open the puckers at the neck. His heart beat hard as he poured the contents on the ground, then he felt a rush of disappointment. Inside were only three dried sticks that resembled those a medicine man sometimes used to tell the future, the arrowhead, and an ancient but perfect Columbia River bird point.

He was about to place the contents back into the bag, when the rattle of parchment told him there was still something in the sack. Reaching in with his forefinger, he drew out a piece of dried summer-weasel hide. Brown and yellowish fur covered one side, but on the parchment side was a map of Oregon and Idaho. Traced in red dye was Uncle Frank's trail across the Oregon desert to his cabin in the Salmon River country of Idaho.

"Mr. Beans!" the boy cried out in excitement. "Uncle Frank has just shown us what to do! We're headed for Idaho, you and I, to Uncle Frank and his cabin, where we'll be safe forever!"

The big bear glanced at the boy, then resumed licking the edges of his wound.

"I'm not sure about the other things in the sack," he said to the bear. "Maybe the little bird point meant I was supposed to take lots of pride in being Indian, and the sticks would help me predict the future, but how will I ever know?

"The map is a big help because it gives us a destination, somewhere to head for. But Uncle Frank didn't know I'd be traveling with a bear. I can't head across the desert through Wagontire and Burns. Folks would see you from miles away. We'd best keep to the Cascades until we come to the Columbia River, then head east to Idaho. That way we could stay in forest most of the way."

Mr. Beans seemed to give in to the excitement in the boy's voice. He reached out with his broad muzzle and licked Chirp's cheek with his rough tongue.

Nine

THEY LEFT THE CAVE BY MOONLIGHT, the boy in the lead, the bear hobbling along behind on three legs. Several times in the past three days, Chirp had tried to lure the bear away, but always, a hundred yards or so from the cave, the animal had stopped and returned to the shelter.

Now, however, Mr. Beans seemed to feel better, and to have developed enough of a dependency on Chirp that he feared being left behind. But still, he traveled as slowly as a grazing cow, pausing frequently to lap up succulent vegetation or turn over a promising rock for small creatures hiding beneath.

The bear had been born on a game farm and raised as a pet, but it wasn't long before he'd picked up the habits of grizzly bears everywhere. While Chirping Bird walked carefully, determined to slip out of the country without leaving signs of their passing, Mr. Beans carelessly created a bulldozer's swath that could have been spotted from the air.

"You don't understand, Mr. Beans!" Chirp grumbled. "Folks might still be looking for us, and if anyone happens on that track you're leaving, they'll have an army after us for sure. You've knocked down so many young trees in the last five miles, it'll look like a hurricane went through."

The grizzly sat down to rip open a rotten log with his one good forepaw, baring a nest of little pink mice, which he licked up as though they were candy. Hurrying on in the midst of such plenty did not seem to be part of the bear's nature. There were still a few scattered ranch houses about and Chirp was impatient to get the animal away from civilization. He wanted Mr. Beans to follow closely at his heels and not decide to pay some rancher a visit.

They skirted a few open fields dotted with cattle. Chirp stayed well back from the fences, hoping to keep the bear from wandering out to investigate, which would have created a stampede of cattle or horses major enough to wake a rancher from his sleep. Sometimes Mr. Beans really seemed to crave his company, following behind as though on an invisible leash. But at other times, the bear completely ignored his pleas to follow. The boy was relieved when they passed beyond the scattered night lights and gained the thicker forests of the Cascades.

For a bear who had lived his life on concrete,

Mr. Beans picked up wilderness living wonderfully well. One morning as they prepared to bed down for the day, the bear sniffed at a hole in the earth, then did what grizzlies have done since time immemorial. He hooked a great paw in the sod and pulled a whole scalp of earth toward his belly, exposing a startled family of ground squirrels, then promptly swatted them to jelly while they were still blinking at the sudden light.

Having devoured this delicacy, the bear was reluctant to join Chirp in hiding, but scalped another piece of turf as big as a country schoolhouse. Sometimes he uncovered mice, gophers, or ground squirrels, but most often, he ended up doing a lot of work for nothing.

Such occasional feasts only made the bear independent. Chirp plunged ahead, trusting that the bear would follow, but usually Mr. Beans ignored his absence and went on feeding. Obviously food took precedence over any social need he had for the boy's company. It was clear to Chirp that they were going to have to proceed to grizzly country in Idaho at the bear's own pace.

Chirp's opportunities for food were far more limited. He robbed every squirrel cache he could find for pine seeds, and boiled nettles, fern fronds, and dandelion greens as a kind of spinach. Much as he liked to eat ipos, the rootlets took some hard digging and generally grew in the clay soil on rock flats where the boy felt exposed to the world.

That night there was a period of pitch darkness

before the moon finally rose over the eastern hills. It was a good time to bed down on a carpet of pine needles to rest while Mr. Beans fed in circles around him. He could hear crackling as logs gave in to the animal's assault, and often he heard the startled alarm calls of a roosting bird as the bear located it with his nose and jerked the whole sapling from underneath it. The bear's shoulder was beginning to heal and he was learning to feed himself. The boy knew that this night was a test of the bear's need for company. He suspected that grizzlies were essentially solitary by nature, and was surprised and pleased when he awoke at dawn and spotted Mr. Beans waiting for him not half a mile away.

The animal no longer seemed hungry and they moved off at a good pace, leaving few tracks. The snowbrush at this elevation was thick, and heavy with the night's dew, and Chirp's pant legs were soon drenched. The land was so peaceful with the approach of day that Chirp almost forgot that they were still on the run, and that danger lurked with every new vista.

From their vantage point on the eastern slope of the Cascades, Chirp could look down and see the great agricultural basin where he had grown up. The vast latticework of irrigation ditches and canals showed silver in the distance, and his glance traced the highway north toward the Indian reservation where he had been born. Highways laced the green valley like cobwebs; he watched in the distance the increasing pulse of traffic as men and women left their houses for work. "I'd better take a good look," Chirp thought. "I may never see the place again."

Still striving to put miles between themselves and their pursuers, the boy kept moving on. Soon a new danger became evident. He first heard the chuffing of a steam locomotive and the rattle of steel on rock as track-laying tractors dragged in logs to be loaded on railroad cars. There was the scraping whine of saws and the occasional crackling and boom of huge trees falling in a cloud of dust. Men were everywhere in the forest: fallers in pairs, cutting down trees with two-man misery whips, choker setters following the tractors on foot to attach cables to logs, scalers running like squirrels over the huge logs to mark the cuts.

From a thicket of lodgepole pine, Chirp gazed out over the scene and planned his next move. Clearly the logging operation extended down the mountain clear to the edge of the north-south highway paralleling the Cascades. If he climbed up above the logging operation, he would be forced to traverse a near-treeless burn where he would be visible for miles. There was one lone neck of timber that had not yet been logged, which would take them north right to where Chirp planned to go. "C'mon, Mr. Beans!" the boy called. When they finally reached the neck of timber, Chirp's heart was pounding with exertion and his lungs hurt from the thin air.

The trees had been marked for cutting but there were no loggers there. They made good time and soon left the logging operation far behind. But ahead of them was a new danger, a busy highway cutting west over the mountains. If they wanted to go north, they would have to figure out a way to cross that highway unseen. Above them on the highway was a convenience store, and beyond that, several habitations.

Chirp moved back into deeper woods to prevent the bear from being spotted by a passing motorist. Somewhere back toward the highway, a dog barked and someone whistled a command. The bear pricked up his ears and looked nervously in the direction of the noise. Using what cover he could find, Chirp climbed higher up the mountain until there were no longer signs of houses.

But now there were horse tracks, not the random wandering of a grazing horse but the hoof-prints of a shod horse systematically patrolling the pumice slopes as though someone were looking for tracks.

Chirp was about to call Mr. Beans and rush across the road when some instinct told him to be careful, that this might be exactly where authorities looking at a map would expect him to try to cross. He sat back against a log, watching the distant traffic flow, trying to determine just how long a lag he could expect between automobiles, and wondering if he should wait for the cover of darkness.

He realized that once before, when he was planning to run away, he had shared his plan with Mugsy. North up the eastern side of the Cascades to the Columbia, then east up the Columbia and Snake to Idaho to try to locate Uncle Frank. Mugsy was always trying to please his father. Maybe he had told the man what Chirp's route would be.

From his hidden vantage point, the boy could watch the road without being seen. Suddenly, from the woods across the highway, sunlight flashed on glass and he heard a car door close. Not a careless slam, but deliberately and softly. Someone was parked there off the highway for no apparent reason, perhaps waiting for the boy and bear to cross.

"Wow!" Chirp breathed. "If I hadn't been careful, I'd have blundered right into a trap!"

Moving back away from the highway, he ran across fresh sneaker tracks and followed them for a few yards, thinking maybe it was some local boy hunting squirrels. Then suddenly the sneaker tracks stopped abruptly at the trail Chirp and the bear had made only an hour ago. Whoever the person was, he had stood a long time in one spot as though examining every detail of their footprints.

"Chirp! Hey, Chirp! It's me, Mugsy, your old pal!"

Chirp spun around to see Mugsy sitting on a stump not forty feet away.

"What are you doing here?" he growled, not at all glad to see the older boy.

"I had to warn you," Mugsy said. "Down the road there a quarter mile, my dad is sittin' in his pickup waitin' for that bear to cross. And further down the road are police cars parked every two hundred yards, just dyin' for a shot. Some logger saw you this mornin' and phoned in a report from that store down the way. It was on the radio. Said you had skirted the loggin' operation and were headin' north with the bear."

Mugsy looked at Chirp hopefully. "I could throw them off the trail!" he suggested. "Tell them I saw the bear cross on up the road. My dad would be after it in a flash, and we could make a run for it between cars."

"We?" Chirp said.

"Yeah, you an' me! We could let that bear fend for himself and take off, spend the summer livin' like Indians in the Cascades. We could rip some of our clothes, yours and mine mixed, so they'd think the bear got us both. Then nobody'd come lookin' fer us. C'mon, Chirpin' Bird. Let's do it!"

Looking at his former friend, Chirp suddenly felt sad for him. In just a few short days of being hunted, he himself had grown up. He was living out a real-life drama. Why would he be interested in going back to silly children's games? Why play with a white boy at being Indian when he WAS an Indian?

"You'd better get out of here fast, Mugsy," he warned, "before that bear catches up. Know what he likes to do with white boys? Eat 'em raw. Like white grubs out of a rotten pine log."

Mugsy looked around the woods for the bear, his eyes showing his fear. He started walking backwards toward the road, tripped, fell over a rotten log, and bounded up. "Come with me," he demanded, his arrogance returning. "This is the best place to cross. It's safe over there! There's nobody watchin' this spot. Honest!"

"You're lying, Mugs!" Chirp called out to him. "Your dad's right over there in those woods. You think I don't know you? You think I'd pal with a coward like you? I'd rather travel with a bear!"

Mugsy's face turned livid with anger. "Go to hell, then!" He rushed across the borrow pit and headed straight across the highway to where Chirp had seen the flash of sunlight on glass.

"We're in big trouble, Mr. Beans!" Chirp called to the bear who was lying in the shade. "Come on, old friend! We're going to make a run for it!"

He waited as a loaded logging truck rumbled west, then rushed across the road, skirting to the right of the spot where Mugsy had disappeared. To his relief the bear stayed right on his heels.

Once he gained the pine thickets, Chirp kept running hard until his breath came in gasps and his sides ached like a green-apple bellyache. Sometimes the bear traveled ahead of him, picking the route; sometimes he followed behind. Even on three legs, the bear could outrun the boy. Every quarter of a mile or so, Chirp doubled back and circled. Mr. Flanigan and Mugsy wouldn't expect him to cross the highway so close to the ambush point, but if pursuers did pick up the trail, such maneuvers would at least buy time.

Far behind them on the highway, Chirp heard

the wail of a police siren, but he had no way of knowing what it meant. If Mugsy had alerted his father, most likely the man would ignore the police and set out on his trail alone. The horse tracks bothered him. Mugsy's father owned a horse trailer and a horse he used in hunting elk. A man on horseback might be hard to elude.

For a time Chirp and the bear followed an old wagon road, but soon it bore heavily west and he had to abandon it and take to the thick brush. Great piles of rock made travel difficult. There were caves galore, but they were too small to give shelter to a bear.

Just before dark he and Mr. Beans found a suitable shelter. Or rather Mr. Beans found it for them, for he was sitting in the entrance as Chirp approached. The bear immediately lost himself in the shadows at the rear of the cave, but Chirp could hear his regular breathing not very far away.

The cave smelled faintly of skunk, and the boy hoped the creature would not pay them a visit during the night. He was hungry, but there was little he could do about finding food before morning.

For a moment he regretted not letting Mugsy come along, just for company. As he sat in the darkness waiting for sleep, he felt lonesome. At least if Mugsy were there he would have someone to talk to and share in this marvelous, if desperate, adventure. A perverse little thought ran through his head and made him smile: if you really want to have a one-way conversation, try talking to a grizzly bear.

Ten

IT SEEMED TO CHIRP that they were always climbing, and that every day the soil was thinner and there were more rocks. But at that elevation, there were no signs of civilization, and he and the big bear shared ownership of a vast and lonely world.

That afternoon the clouds descended upon them and left the vegetation wet and cold. The bear's wound was healing well along the edges of its massive scab of pitch and pine needles. But the grizzly seemed perpetually hungry and spent much time foraging for food.

Now and then the boy found an abandoned deer-hunting camp and marveled at the useful things hunters left behind. Once it was a rusty hunting knife left sticking in a tree; commonly there were chunks of hemp rope and old, battered cooking pots that were better than his tin cans. And often there were caches of dried food sealed in cans and jars to save packing it in the next year.

Usually it was Mr. Beans who foraged on ahead and found the food first. Then the boy had to rush in fast to keep the bear from breaking jars and ripping open storage cans, spilling the contents over half an acre of ground.

All those jumbled rocks fallen from volcanic peaks usually meant there were caves or overhangs that gave them a roof to sleep under. Mr. Beans was still out foraging when the boy found shelter under a ledge of gray lava and built a tiny fire. He was careful not to choose a spot out in the open where it might be seen for miles and attract the attention of fire lookouts who watched over this whole vast land each summer.

For some time he worked in the shelter, hulling pine nuts by rubbing them against one another and winnowing out the hulls in the wind. He tossed the nuts repeatedly in the air, letting the wind blow the lighter chaff away, then caught them in an old rusty piece of window screen he'd found in a deer camp.

That night the clouds brought darkness early, and Chirp made a bed of soft sand next to the rocky wall and tried to sleep. He was soon cold, and there seemed no way to escape those damp high-elevation winds that explored the shallow shelter.

Knees against his chest, he tried in vain to warm himself, but his wet feet turned icy and he shivered and shook. For a few hours he slept in fitful naps, miserable in his bed, then, suddenly, it was as though someone had placed a nice warm fur robe against his body.

Chirp came awake in a hurry. The bear was lying against him, protecting him as if he were a cub. As the grizzly muttered to himself, he seemed to hum or groan a tune known only to bears. For some time Chirp lay enjoying the warmth but hoping the bear would not roll over and crush him. Finally Chirp's shivering stopped and he slept.

When dawn finally came, the bear was still lying beside him. Sensing that the boy was awake, the bear turned his head sideways to be scratched. Chirp reached out and fingered the bear's stubby ears.

"Oooooooooah," the big animal rumbled in ecstasy, closing his eyes.

"Now how do I stop without making Mr. Beans sore at me?" the boy wondered.

The bear solved that problem himself, for suddenly the demands of hunger seemed to take over. Mr. Beans lumbered to his feet and limped off to look for food. When the boy was finally forced from his bed by the cold, Mr. Beans was already a quarter of a mile down the slope, tearing apart a rotten fir log for grubs.

For a few minutes, Chirp sat soaking up the early morning sunshine, thinking how lucky he was to be here along the crest of the Cascades, and appreciating the experience of being accepted by the bear. A Canada jay silently flew over to investigate the camp for crumbs, and perched, gray feathers fluffed, on a dead snag. It cocked its head and regarded the boy quizzically. Chirp wished he had something to feed the visitor, but his larder was bare.

"Sorry, Mr. Jay," he apologized. "Things have been a little lean lately. You travel with a hungry bear an' you don't get to lay up much for hard times. What you don't gulp down on the spot, Mr. Beans cleans up for you, then does the dishes and licks the pot to boot."

The jay seemed to accept his explanation and went winging off, looking perhaps for a more productive camp.

A few hundred yards north of the shelter, a tumbling mountain stream, fed by melting snows above the tree line, frothed and gurgled its way down the slopes toward civilization. Chirp walked over to inspect the clear pools for trout but saw not even a water bug. At this elevation the water was too pure and cold.

The bear was busy getting his breakfast down in a meadow, so Chirp took time out for a bath. He stripped off his worn, dusty clothes, washed them, and lay them out on rocks to dry, then scrubbed himself clean. The cold water took his breath away, but when he came plunging out of the stream, the mountain sun beat down on his brown body and chased away the goose bumps. He stretched out to dry on a flat gray lava rock that was already warm from the sun.

As Chirp lay taking a sunbath, the bear wandered up the hillside and found Chirp's clothes on the rocks. He sniffed them carefully as though trying to figure out what had happened to his friend. When Chirp sat up laughing, Mr. Beans stood on his hind legs, staring, dropped to his feet, whirled, charged down the slope, then turned again to face the strange human. "Whuff!" he snorted in alarm.

"Hey, Mr. Beans. It's only me! See, I can put my fur on or take it off!"

As the bear circled downwind, trying to catch his scent, Chirp dressed quickly, not caring to be around a frightened grizzly. Only when he was fully dressed did the bear dare approach the boy. After sniffing Chirp from head to toe, he seemed satisfied that his friend was back and ambled off down the hillside without a backward glance.

Under a deadfall Chirp found a snowshoe hare that still wore a few patches of unshed winter hair mixed with the brown of its summer coat. The boy crept close, instinctively knowing he must be careful not to alarm the animal with eye contact. He killed it with a stick, then cleaned it with his hunting knife and boiled it over a small fire. He was relieved to see that the wind took the faint blue haze of smoke and scattered it across the hillside.

Once the meat was cooked, he ate it hurriedly, frequently glancing down the slope to keep an eye out for the bear, who might catch the meal's fragrance on the wind and challenge him for it. He didn't mind sharing with the grizzly, but he knew that the bear would have no such feelings. One bite and the hare would be gone, and Mr. Beans would ransack the area, looking for more.

For a few hours, the boy and the bear searched for plainer food on the rocky hillsides. Chirp ate cress from streams, picked dandelion greens, and searched for caches of seeds and pine nuts hidden by squirrels.

Now and again, as he tore apart rotten logs looking for treasure troves of nuts, he found great, white, waxy boreworm grubs. Mugsy once told Chirp he'd read that some tribes ate them like candy, but Chirp had a long way to go before he could accept his ancestral diet completely. Instead he gathered all he could find and fed them to Mr. Beans.

For more than an hour, the bear grazed like a cow on succulent green forbs along the streams, pausing now and then to scrape a promising area for voles and pocket gophers. Often these scrapes were big enough to be seen by small planes flying fire patrol, so the boy dragged in brush, trying his best to cover the bear's activity.

He was relieved when Mr. Beans seemed to want to head north again, exploring thick forests of fir, western white pine, and mountain hemlock. An airplane would have to be directly overhead to detect their passing. That day they made over fifteen miles, and it was dark when they bedded down near another stream.

Since they could not find a proper shelter in the dark, the bear chose a hollow next to a giant windfall. Careful not to bump the bear's sore shoulder, Chirp leaned up against the sleeping animal and soon was lost to the world.

A pair of gray jays wakened them at dawn. The birds called down plaintively at the sleeping pair. As Chirp struggled to the stream to wash the sleep from his eyes, he found an ancient blade of shiny black obsidian lying on the bank, distinctively shaped, as sharp and delicate as though some Indian had made it yesterday and left it here for him to discover.

"Look at this, Mr. Beans!" he called. "Look at the skinning knife I found!"

He cradled the precious blade in his hands, then took his white man's knives and buried them in the same sandy bank where he had found the artifact. He sensed that the Indian who had made the knife was there, hovering about him, pleased that he would put the knife to good use dressing out game.

Having wrapped the sharp obsidian carefully in dry grass, he placed it in his pack and began to move north again, crossing the stream on a handy log as the bear splashed noisily through.

Edging around a rocky tumble of lava rocks, Chirp and the bear suddenly froze in their tracks as a piercing whistle startled them, but it was only a fat old marmot sunning himself on the rocks. The boy hungered for marmot roasted over a fire, but he knew that the animal had plenty of tunnels to safety and would disappear the moment they headed his way.

As they topped the next ridge, they looked down into a broad, timbered basin dotted with blue lakes.

"Trouble ahead, Mr. Beans!" the boy said.

"Those lakes have to be full of fish, and this time of year the shores will be hip-to-hip with folks camping. Getting you past those camps will be like telling a three-year-old kid not to sample merchandise in a candy store!"

Chirp tried to skirt the area by hugging the steep rock slides high above the lakes, but the going was tough. Winter snows had avalanched, taking the trees with them and leaving naked barrens where a hundred pair of eyes could have marked their passing.

They had just descended one long hillside to climb another, when suddenly, the boy heard a snort and the ringing of steel on rock as shod horses clambered for footing. Below them a pack train of two dozen horses and mules scrambled in confusion as they looked up the ridge at the bear.

"Whooooah there, you hosses! Whooooah!" a cowboy roared, reining up his plunging horse.

Mr. Beans uttered a loud "whoooof" and stood up on his hind legs for a better look.

Climbing over one another in sheer terror, bucking and snorting, the pack animals slid off the steep trail and went tumbling down the hillside, scattering packs, groceries, cameras, pots, pans, tents, and bedrolls as they fell. Horses reared and plunged, throwing their riders into the brush before stampeding back down the mountain.

Mr. Beans moved forward for a better look, and Chirp heard a scream as a young woman fell off her horse. She clutched a young sapling as she slid to the ground, tried to pull herself to her feet, then fainted. The other folks Chirp could see were strictly taking care of themselves, running over one another down the trail as if the grizzly were right on their heels.

The bear crawled over a fallen log and found himself face-to-face with a frightened cowboy, who held up one arm as though to fend off the bear's charge, then jumped up and followed his pack string down the mountain, leaving the girl where she had fallen. Chirp was relieved to see the young lady stagger to her feet, leaving her bonnet hanging from a tree, and make tracks down the mountain on her own.

"I knew these days were too peaceful to last, Mr. Beans," Chirp groaned. "Let's get out of here fast while we've got a chance!"

But the big bear had scented food and was soon sitting happily in the midst of spilled groceries, ripping open packs of meat and smashing canned goods with his teeth to let the sweet fruity syrup dribble down his jaws.

"C'mon!" Chirp yelled as he rushed on past. "You dumb old bear! We're in real trouble now! Whoever comes back to investigate will find bear tracks all over the place, and those big teeth marks on the cans will tell them all they want to know about who caused this ruckus!"

He grabbed a frying pan, a fine big tin of ham, and some smaller cans as spoils of war, and rushed on, leaving the bear to satisfy his hunger.

For a time he ran from pool to pool down the rocky stream, hoping to hide his footprints. He clutched the tins and the frying pan as though his life depended upon them, not daring to look back to see if anyone was following. He heard splashing behind him and turned, fearing pursuit, but it was only the bear plunging along, carrying a chunk of beef in his jaws.

Leaving the stream when it disappeared into the steep of a canyon, he sought out some rock flats where trackers would have a tough time picking up their trail. It was only when they were high up on the next ridge that he stopped to look back at the scene of the carnage.

"We're in big trouble! Look back there! Must be a hundred people milling around. We almost had it made when you spooked that pack train. It won't be long before the law is fresh on our trail again. We'd best cross over to the west side of the Cascades and hope for rain to wash out our tracks. It's our only chance."

For a time the bear seemed almost contrite and kept up with the boy, but just when Chirp thought that maybe he had learned a lesson, Mr. Beans chased a cottontail rabbit into a burrow and proceeded to scalp a dozen square yards of turf trying to find the elusive animal. Only when the boy disappeared over a ridge did the bear decide to follow.

That night they made camp under a good overhanging rock. The bear seemed restless, and Chirp built a corral of heavy rocks around the animal. But they were not heavy enough, for in the morning the bear was gone and the rocks were scattered where he had pushed them aside. Chirp had slept so soundly he had not even heard Mr. Beans leave.

Already a hot mountain sun was beating down on the rocky hillside. He gave the alarm whistle of a marmot, hoping that the bear would look up from his feeding or even stand up on his hind legs so he could detect the animal's whereabouts. But the only response to his whistle came from a pair of Clark's nutcrackers, who answered the alarm with one of their own.

From the tracks Chirp decided that the bear must have gone back to where the pack train had wrecked.

"You fool!" the boy muttered. "You danged stupid bear! That place will still be alive with people ready to hunt you down." He set off on the bear's trail, aware that with every step he was undoing the labored flight of yesterday.

He had gone only a mile when he heard a fusillade of shots in the distance. A small dot appeared on the horizon of Chirp's world, getting larger and larger as it sped toward him. It was Mr. Beans, running for dear life as spent bullets ripped up the dust behind him.

Chirp turned and ran in the same direction as the bear, grateful for the roughness of the terrain and the fields of shattered lava that were his only hope to keep the trackers off their trail.

Eleven

THE LIGHTNING STORM CAME out of nowhere one evening and hammered the forest about them without mercy, leaving a string of small fires like a ruby necklace about the throat of the mountain. Fortunately there was not a lot of combustible material at that high elevation, but Chirp still knew that fire lookout towers would be phoning in locations of strikes on their single-wire, ground-return phone lines, and that even while the storm still raged, fire reconnaissance planes would be on their way to monitor the blazes.

"C'mon, Mr. Beans!" Chirp said, gathering up his cans and cookware. "This old mountain isn't going to stay ours for very long!"

The storm was making the big bear nervous and it was hard for the boy to get the animal to leave the shelter of the windfall, but as Chirp disappeared over the first ridge, the grizzly got lonesome and came ambling after him.

Chain lightning kept the mountainside bright as day, and the shortest strands of the boy's hair stood up straight with electricity. He avoided tall trees, especially those on the ridges, and sought out areas where brush and saplings made less of a target.

Downslope a tall snag was afire at its base and the flames were licking up the sides, fueled by an accumulation of yellow pitch. A tower of black smoke stood higher than the mountain peaks, then flattened against an invisible stratum of upper air until it resembled a giant mushroom.

"Hurry, Mr. Beans!" the boy shouted over the roar of flames and thunder. "We've got to get out of here! And fast!"

Somewhere in the storm he could hear the sound of a light plane and wondered how it could possibly avoid being struck down by lightning.

Chirp kept longing for rain, a deluge that would put out the fires and send the plane winging back to civilization, but none came. Descending a gully in the occasional darkness between lightning flashes, he fell and scraped his knee against a sharp rock, and the utensils and grub he carried in his pack went flying. He had to wait for another series of flashes to see well enough to pick up his belongings.

The ordeal left him exhausted, but at last he tied up his precious cargo in his pack and moved forward again. "Just a little bit further, Mr. Beans," he called into the darkness. "Just a little bit further and we'll find us a nice windfall where we can rest."

For two hours they pushed ahead, and still the dry parallel lightning lit the sky. Chirp's knee pained him with every step, but he kept on, afraid that by morning the hillsides would be swarming with firefighters. His eyelids felt thick and heavy and stung with acrid smoke; as he staggered on, he kept falling asleep on his feet.

They were almost out of the fire area and were crossing a small rocky clearing when a fire plane came sweeping over the ridge, flying low above the edge of the flat. Chirp prayed for darkness, but just as the plane flew past, a brilliant burst of lightning illuminated boy and bear and exposed them for one agonizingly long moment to the pilot.

"He saw us, Mr. Beans! I know he saw us! Danged old lightning anyway! I expect right now he's headed back to a landing strip to phone in to his dispatcher that he spotted us. Tomorrow the newspapers will be full of it and Mugsy's dad will have a new fix on where we are and have it all figured out just where we are going to pass!"

Twelve

CHIRP AND MR. BEANS spent the rest of the night sleeping in a patch of snowbrush beside a fallen ponderosa pine. Even though he was exhausted, the boy slept fitfully. All through the night he could hear the rumble and crash of trucks and the clank and screech of tracklayers as the fire control people moved in equipment and personnel to fight the fires.

He reasoned that even if the pilot of that fire plane had turned in a report of a boy and a bear heading over the crest of the Cascades, the fires were going to take priority, and only when the fires were out would anyone come searching for their trail. But that did not include Mr. Flanigan, who could load his horse into his trailer and be there within two hours.

Whatever Chirp and Mr. Beans did, it must not

be the predictable. On one side of the mountain range were tinder-dry conditions and forest fires. On the other a moist fog was blowing off the Pacific Ocean, and the woods, even in summer, were cool and damp. Ahead of them stretched a wild country, much of which was steep as a cow's face.

Up to now, like the early explorers, he had surveyed the terrain up ahead and taken the easiest way. But this time, because of Mr. Flanigan and the threat of being ambushed, he had to take the safe way, which was, of course, the way no one would expect them to travel.

Dawn came up crimson, blushing through a haze of smoke stretching east over the far-off Oregon desert. As they slid down the western slope of the mountains, the wet vegetation soaked them both and the brush caught at Chirp's legs and held him back. In every valley a torrent of icy water tumbled west toward the Pacific. The streams were a welcome source of water, but the boy grew tired of walking extra miles to find a crossing log. If anyone followed them through this hell, he was going to earn every foot of the trail. A cold drizzling rain made travel even more miserable, and Mr. Beans added to the misery by shaking the moisture from his fur and drenching the boy in the process.

For two days Chirp fought the western slope, then gave up and crossed through a narrow pass to the arid eastern side again. Below them Chirp could see a blue mountain lake stretching for several miles across their path. Beyond the lake a dusty highway cut up over the mountains. The boy sat perched on a rock and wondered which route made the most sense.

If Mr. Flanigan intended to ambush them, the man would probably choose the area between the lake and the logged-over area farther east. Chirp thought he might have a better chance if he descended the mountains altogether and dropped down to the lodgepole pine thickets for which there was no commercial use, which meant no logging.

Far below he noticed a pickup truck, pulling a horse trailer, navigating a skein of old logging roads and leaving a trail of dust that drifted high over the forest. He waited until the truck had disappeared east over the ridges before he began his descent, pausing every now and then to wait for Mr. Beans to finish tearing open a rotten log.

Down on the flat, a series of small beaver dams impounded a small stream, and here the boy stopped to bathe while the bear cavorted about, trying in vain to capture the small trout that darted between his legs.

Chirp lay on his stomach along a cut bank and dangled his fingers in the cold water, feeling carefully beneath the bank until he found the smooth, soft belly of a large trout. He grinned with satisfaction. The trout wasn't his yet, but it would be. Slowly, careful not to alarm the fish, he began stroking its belly. Twice the trout left the cover of the bank to swim briefly out into the current, and Chirp feared he had lost the fish forever, but both times the trout returned to the shadows beneath the bank. The boy let the trout rest a moment to feel safe, then once more began to stroke its underside.

"Don't hurry it, boy!" Uncle Frank's voice seemed to be telling him. "Tickling a trout takes lots of patience. Take your time till that old trout gets sort of hypnotized, then work your fingers slowly, slowly, up to its gills and wham! You got it!"

Chirp wished the old man were here beside him now. What a time the three of them could have together!

Chirp went back to his tickling. The trout's belly was heavy from feasting on recent insect hatches. Back and forth his fingers went. His hand was getting numb from the cold water, but he kept up the action. Carefully he worked his fingers up into the trout's gills and closed them. Pow! He jerked the fish out from under the bank and threw it wriggling and flopping onto the grass.

He glanced around quickly for Mr. Beans, but the bear had batted ashore a good fish of his own and held it crossways in his mouth as he moved off into the brush. Chirp gutted out his fish with the black obsidian knife, marveling at the sharpness of the blade, then roasted the fish on green sticks over a willow fire. Even without salt, he thought, he had never tasted anything so delicious.

In the distance he heard the rumble of a truck and saw the top of the vehicle as it passed not a quarter of a mile away. Maybe someone had seen his smoke from higher up, but he couldn't be sure.

Mr. Beans was lying flat in the water now, soaking his shoulder, so he didn't have to worry about the bear being seen.

He carried a pot of water to the fire and doused the embers carefully, then turned and moved off down the hill. "Hurry up, Mr. Beans!" he called as the bear rose dripping from the pond and followed after. Like some big, waterlogged golden retriever, the bear waited until he was beside the boy to shake himself dry.

"Quit that!" Chirp snapped, more harshly than he intended.

Mr. Beans sat down on his haunches and regarded the boy for a moment with sad little eyes, and Chirp moved to the big wet bear and gave the animal a hug. "I'm sorry, Mr. Beans. I was still kind of cold from catching that trout and—well, maybe I do have a short fuse lately, but I'm worried. You go prancing along like you could care less that Mugsy's father is out there ahead of us with a rifle, just waiting to do us in. Me, I've got to do the worrying for both of us!"

The bear lifted a hind paw and licked it carefully. A small, sharp stick had become embedded in the flesh beside the pad, and Chirp reached over and pulled it out.

"Ya know?" Chirp said, trying to make up for his snappishness. "We travel together pretty darn well, you and I. Sometimes you go wandering off by yourself for hours and I think I'll never see you again, then I hear a sound behind me and there you are right on my tail, with your nose down following my tracks."

The boy stroked the massive hump of muscle and fat over the bear's shoulders, then tickled the big animal's stubby ears. The bear closed his eyes in contentment. The hot sun birthed a small whirlwind in a nearby clearing and it took off through the forest, scattering dead manzanita leaves and pine needles as it passed.

The bear's long guard hairs dried quickly and stood up straight, making him appear much larger than when he was wet. "Whoof!" the bear sneezed, sending a chipmunk downslope from them scurrying for cover.

They had traveled across lodgepole pine flats for less than half a mile when Chirp stopped suddenly and listened. Something wasn't right! It was much too silent to be natural. Even the birds had stopped singing! He dropped to his knees in the brush, and the bear sat down quietly, panting in the heat, and seemed to listen with him.

The bear heard the sound first and honed in on its location, focusing on a thicket to the right of them, then lifting his muzzle slightly to catch a scent. Chirp heard it, too. Someone was sobbing. Someone lost, scared, and out of control.

The big grizzly picked out a piece of shade, lay down quietly, and seemed to blend in with the volcanic sand.

"Stay here," Chirp whispered. "I'll go take a look."

The boy moved stealthily through the brush, careful not to snap a dry twig. The sobbing broke out afresh a little farther to the right than he had first thought. Chirp tried to peer over the top of a fallen log, but could see nothing.

Like an animal the Indian boy circled downwind, listening carefully, alert to ambush from all sides. Far off a Townsend's solitaire called plaintively once, twice, and was silent.

Suddenly the sobbing began again, and Chirp saw movement. Mugsy Flanigan sat on a stump, face in his hands, crying his heart out! Chirp muttered to himself in anger.

"Mugsy!" he whispered. "What on earth is he up to now?"

Thirteen

CHIRP DROPPED TO HIS KNEES behind a log, peering about for Mugsy's father, expecting to see him step from behind a tree at any moment with rifle blazing. He glanced back on his trail, but Mr. Beans must have been still snoozing. Sobbing, the white boy sat on his log, pausing occasionally to mop his eyes.

The Indian boy wasted no time with formalities. "Where's your old man, Mugsy?"

Mugsy jumped, spun around, lost his balance, and fell backwards off the log.

"Chirp! Boy, am I glad to see you!" he cried, crawling to his feet. He had one arm in a sling now and pulled himself up gingerly as though protecting it. The scars appeared to have healed long ago, and Chirp thought maybe Mugsy was wearing the sling because people were running out of sympathy.

"I'll bet you're glad," Chirp said. "Where's your old man hiding?"

"Honest, Chirp, I don't know. He took me along yesterday to drive the pickup and horse trailer while he searched for you ahorseback. A fire plane spotted you and the bear crossing over west of the Cascades, but he figured you wouldn't last long in all that wet. He saw you and the bear through his binoculars as you headed back through a pass to the eastern slope, but it was too far for a shot."

The boy wiped his nose on his dirty sleeve and went on. "Yesterday about noon I dropped the old man off with his horse about fifteen miles back and was supposed to pick them up along the road at dark. He took all the food with him and I got hungry. I left the pickup and trailer on a logging spur and was looking for some berries to eat when I got lost. Had to spend the night in the woods. If he ever catches up to me, he's goin' to kill me!" Mugsy struggled to his feet and grabbed Chirp by the arm. "Please, Chirp, you gotta take me along!"

"No way!"

"Chirp! I can help! Dang you, you never were long on brains. If you've still got that bear with you, I can get you both so far away from here, the law won't know where to look."

Chirping Bird looked interested. "How you going to do that?"

"We've got to find the pickup first. Then we load your old bear in the horse trailer and take off. The old man will think I'm still lost. It will be days before they stop looking for me on these loggin' roads." He seemed to notice how thin and lean Chirp had become. "I happen to have some money on me," he said. "First town we come to we could stop and get a burger. With cheese and onions. How about a banana split? An' somethin' for the bear."

Chirp sat down on a log to think. Mugsy had betrayed him before. What if it were a setup? Maybe Mugsy just wanted to get in good with his dad. What if Old Man Flanigan were hiding in the brush by the trailer? Once the bear was loaded, the man could step up and shoot the grizzly point-blank. And what would a madman like Flanigan do to witnesses? Probably shoot them both on the spot!

"It'll work, Chirp! Honest! No tricks! I got a stake in getting away from the old man, too."

Chirp rose to his feet and took his pack. "No promises," he said. "Show me your tracks up on the ridge and I'll at least help you find your truck."

Mugsy looked around cautiously. "The bear! I don't see it. You still travelin' with it?"

Chirp nodded. "He'll be along when he's good and ready."

Already his sharp eyes had picked up the white boy's clumsy trail and he began to follow it through the thickets, letting Mugsy keep up as best he could.

As they circled a small clearing, the bear caught up to them. Mugsy nearly jumped out of his skin when he looked back to see the big animal nosing along on their trail. Mr. Beans paid no more attention to the boy than if he were invisible. The huge animal passed him and shuffled on ahead, trailing at Chirp's heels.

"There it is!" Mugsy said as though he were the one who had found the way out of the woods.

The pickup truck and high-walled wooden horse trailer stood parked beside a small logging spur about half a mile off the main road. Chirp ordered the older boy to stay by the bear while he made a circle, looking for Mr. Flanigan's tracks. He felt better when he found nothing to indicate that the man had been there. Maybe Mugsy was playing it straight for once. Chirp was tired of plowing through the underbrush, and the chance to put in some fast miles toward Idaho seemed worth a risk.

"How are you going to get the bear to load?" Mugsy asked as Chirp opened the rear door of the big four-horse rig.

"Easy!" Chirp replied, enjoying his new position of superiority. From his pack he took the big tin of ham he had been hoarding since they had upset the pack train and twisted the key to open the top. Mr. Beans smelled the treat from a hundred feet away where he had been searching for grubs in a stump. He ambled over, sniffing the air as he came.

"In," Chirp commanded as though he were used to giving the bear orders. The bear had been hauled before, by Diamond Sally, and followed Chirp into the rig.

Moments later, with Mugsy driving and the bear

well hidden by the high walls of the trailer, they rattled off the forest road onto pavement. If Mugsy's account were to be trusted, they were leaving Mr. Flanigan riding his horse on a cold trail somewhere miles behind.

Mugsy seemed elated, as close to his old self as he had been since the night they counted coup on the bear. He tore the sling off his arm and chucked it behind the back seat of the truck. "I wore it to get out of work," he explained. "It's funny," he mused. "Never thought I'd be tootlin' north through Oregon with a bear behind!"

Fourteen

THAT NIGHT THEY CAMPED IN THE WOODS far off the main road and away from the sounds of traffic. Once the bear had grazed, he came back to finish what was left of the huge sack of fries and hamburgers Mugsy had bought at a cafe, and then lay down to sleep with his back against the trailer as though he owned it. Mugsy slept in the seat of the pickup while Chirp stretched out beside the bear.

Chirp could have slept better, but an image of Uncle Frank kept invading his dreams. The old Indian twisted the beak of his cap nervously as he talked. "You be careful, you hear? That white boy claims to be your friend but he'd do anything to please his old man."

The next morning the bear stepped into the trailer easily and lay down in the front where there was less wind. They filled the pickup truck tank with gas at a country service station. Mugsy paid for it with cash from his father's wallet, which he'd found in the glove compartment. From what Chirp could see, there seemed to be a good supply.

There was not much traffic on the road and the boys made good time. At noon they stopped at a highway eatery for food and more gas.

A Greyhound bus drove up while they were still parked at the pump and a host of tired tourists filed into the little café to eat. The bus driver, however, stayed by his bus, smoking a cigarette. He was a fat man, wearing a bright shirt that curved with his belly. He sported dark glasses and a jaunty visored cap with a badge pinned to the front.

He sauntered over to the boys as though he had a need of talking.

"Whatcha got in the trailer, kiddos? A horse?"

He was about to peer over the slats in the trailer door when Chirp blocked his view.

"Nothing yet, mister. We're on our way to the stockyards to pick up some hogs the old man bought at the sale."

"You Injun?"

"Nez Perce," Chirp replied, trying to hold back his irritation. He wished the fat driver would load his fat tourists into his fat bus and drive away.

Someone indoors put money in a jukebox, and the air was filled with a lively polka. The trailer shifted as Mr. Beans woke up, rose heavily to his feet, and began to dance. "Oh, no!" Chirp muttered as the trailer started to rock.

The man did not appear to notice the movement, but as he went into the café to call out his passengers, Chirp saw him glance at the truck's license plate as though committing the numbers to memory.

"Let's scram out of here!" Chirp said as Mugsy brought out sandwiches and pop. "That was a close one. Thought that bus driver was going to crawl up the side of the trailer and take a look. And when that music came on, Mr. Beans began dancing around as though he was doing a number with Miss Sally."

As they drove through the small town, Chirp kept glancing at the speedometer. "Hey, watch it, Mugs! The speed limit here is fifteen miles an hour. If we get stopped for speeding, it will be all over fast."

"They'll never take my license away though," Mugsy grinned.

"Why not?" Chirp asked.

"'Cause I don't have one!"

For a moment Mugsy proceeded at a crawl.

Chirp glanced in the rearview mirror and saw a police car following about two blocks back. He tensed, but the car turned off at an intersection and was gone. He eyed Mugsy's face carefully, wondering if he could really trust him, or if he had a plan. The boy was driving safely enough, but all he had to do was pull some bonehead violation and the police would have them. Most likely the bear would be killed and Chirp would be taken back to Calamity Falls as a runaway.

"Slow down!" Chirp snapped as Mugsy speeded up near the edge of town. "Can't you read? The sign back there said thirty miles an hour and you're going forty."

"Sorry," Mugsy said, but this time he didn't slow down.

Soon they were out of the farming areas and back on the open road. Where there was irrigation, the land was productive, but without water, the scenery was rocky, arid, and colored camel-hair tan. But there was little traffic, and Chirp allowed himself to daydream. He wondered what Idaho would be like. Mountains and big trees. Rich ranches. And lakes. Lots of lakes with trout in them, just waiting to be caught. He couldn't wait to see Uncle Frank and tell him all that had happened.

He could still remember the old man's stories. There wasn't any place in the state that Uncle Frank hadn't been. Helped some rancher once take a herd of cows into the Salmon River backcountry. Said the mosquitoes were so thick they sucked all the blood out of the cattle and the cows got so thin you could see daylight right through them. Uncle Frank swore they sold a few of them to homesteaders along the way for lampshades.

He wished Uncle Frank was with them now. He'd be able to read Mugsy like a book. He tried to picture the old man as he'd last seen him, restless to be off to Idaho but full of fun and tales. Mostly he remembered the cap, and the twinkle in his eye as he started telling a story, twisting the brim of his hat round and round.

"Hey!" Chirp said sharply. "Keep her down to about fifty!"

"I'm drivin'," the older boy snapped. "Don't be so danged cranky. Without me you'd still be back there in the woods."

Along the edge of the Warm Springs Indian Reservation, they pulled off the road when Chirp spotted an elderly Indian trying to change a flat tire on his Model A pickup. It seemed safe enough, since the road was dusty and desolate. As usual Chirp did all the work while Mugsy stood by giving advice.

The old man smelled of sagebrush smoke. His eyes were red-rimmed, black and bottomless, with turkey-track wrinkles in the corners. His voice was guttural. Like so many older Indians Chirp knew, he exhaled as he talked, pushing out the words. "Jus' heard on the radio," he said. "Jus' heard on the radio cops lookin' fer a new pickup truck jus' lak yours."

"Oh?" Chirp said, pretending not to care.

"Pullin' a wooden horse trailer jus' lak yours."

"Lotsa rigs like ours on the road," Mugsy said. "Musta passed a dozen or so this mornin'."

"Funny t'ing. Cops, they lookin' fer a couple of boys jus' your age!" The old man kept chuckling to himself as Chirp put on the last of the lug nuts, smacked the little hubcap into place, and released the jack.

The old man shook both their hands warmly. "You boys was plenny nice to stop to help this old

Indian." His eyes twinkled playfully. "Ennybody ask, I din't see you two boys. Or the pickup. Or that wooden trailer, you hear? No sirree, I din't see you two boys. Or the bear!"

Soon they were back on the road, but Chirp had been warned. Mr. Flanigan had evidently made it out of the woods and found out that his son had run off with the pickup, horse trailer, Chirp, and the bear. It must have been a shock to Mr. Flanigan—unless it was all part of a plan. Chirp resolved that the first good chance he got, he would leave Mugsy behind and proceed on foot.

Fifteen

For a time Chirp fell asleep, lulled by the hum of the tires. When he awoke, it was as though they had come to the end of the world.

"Pull over!" Chirp said suddenly, ordering the older boy to leave the pavement for a graveled area above the Columbia River Valley.

As Mugsy pulled over and parked on the overlook, both boys sat spellbound at the sight.

"Wow! Look at that water! That's Washington State on the other side!" Mugsy said as though he didn't expect Chirp to know.

The boys got out of the pickup and stretched. Chirp pretended that he was just interested in scenery, but his mind was abuzz with the reality of that river. He had envisioned a big bridge crossing the Columbia that would take him to the Washington side, but there wasn't a bridge to be seen. There were some huge boats that looked like car ferries, but he had no idea how to find where they docked or just how safe it would be to try to smuggle the bear to the other side of the river.

There were other things that bothered Chirp, too. The whole trip lately had been too easy. Nobody had challenged them. Maybe, Chirp thought, the police have figured that we are heading across the Columbia, and since there can't be that many ferries or bridges, all they have to do is wait around here for a 1940 pickup pulling a horse trailer.

Chirp glanced at Mugsy, but the boy seemed innocent enough. He was looking off across the fields with his dad's binoculars as though watching for birds. Chirp felt a chill go through him. What if this whole thing had been planned beforehand? What if Mugsy's dad didn't want the police interfering and had set up this whole plan with his son to deliver the bear to a certain point where he could kill Mr. Beans without anyone knowing? Once they drove down that hill, they would run out of options. No more lonely country roads or thick forests in which to hide.

A blue sedan, maybe a '35 or a '36 Chevy, passed them, heading down the hill toward the valley floor. Perhaps he was getting paranoid, but Chirp thought a driver would have glanced their way. Instead the man stared straight ahead down the road.

Chirp picked up Mugsy's binoculars and glassed the river.

"Hey, what are you doin' with those?" Mugsy asked. "Those belong to my dad. He wouldn't want anyone but me to use them."

Chirp ignored him. For a time a bank of dirty gray fog obscured the river and the boats. Then, as it swirled and lifted, he saw what he had been hoping for. A freight train was heading east along the Columbia. He watched as the entire train was swallowed by a tunnel, then emerged, undigested, out of the steep hillside.

Chirp's head was full of ideas, and staying with Mugsy wasn't one of them. More and more he felt Mugsy was up to something. Chirp raised the binoculars again. He desperately needed that train to carry him to Idaho, but there was one major problem. The railroad was on the north side of the river, and he had no way to get across with the bear.

He studied the scene carefully. Evidently the only way over the river at this point was by ferry. For a moment he watched what were probably pro-duce trucks heading east and west along the Columbia. Even with binoculars the big trucks looked like ants traveling both ways on a trail, not even pausing to touch feelers.

The bear began to rock the trailer, impatient to be gone.

"Take it easy, Mr. Beans," Chirp called.

He glanced at Mugsy, looking for some sign of betrayal. The older boy was walking back and forth nervously, but then he was usually nervous.

The blue sedan came up the hill, heading back

116

the way it had come. Again the driver ignored them.

Mugsy glanced at his watch. "We'd better go," he said. "We can drive the pickup and trailer onto the ferry and be in Washington before you know it."

"Who said anything about crossing over to Washington?" Chirp said. "Maybe I wanted to head up the river. Or even down."

Chirp could tell from Mugsy's eyes that he was doing some serious thinking. "I want to go across to Washington," Mugsy said. "My dad took me across on the ferry once on our way to Canada. They raise lots of fruit over there, and when our money gets low, we can get jobs picking apples." He looked once more at his watch. "C'mon," he said. "We gotta go!"

Chirp let the big bear out of the trailer.

"What are you doin'?" Mugsy demanded. "You crazy or somethin'?"

Chirp ignored the older boy. There was a gully leading down the mountain, bridged by the winding road. He made a leash and collar of rope for Mr. Beans and led him into the brush. The big animal seemed ready and eager to dance, as though Miss Sally were just around the corner. "Steady, Mr. Beans," Chirp cautioned. "There are too many people in this neck of the woods to let you run free."

"Walk 'round here like you're stretching your legs," he ordered the older boy. "We'll head into the canyon and wait for you where it makes that big bend."

"I think—" Mugsy started to protest, but Chirp and the bear had already disappeared into the pines and scrub oaks.

For a time it was rough going, but once they had crossed under the highway, they moved easily down the steep hill. Chirp waited at the bend of the canyon, not really wanting Mugsy to show up, but there he was suddenly, puffing with exertion, his shirt torn and a streak of blood across one cheek where a branch had whipped across his face.

"Maybe it's better," Chirp thought, "to have him where I can see him." Soon he cut back up the wall of the canyon and into a heavy strip of forest that led west along the shoulders of the valley. Now and then he paused and watched the river, fascinated by the white water splaying from the faster boats, and the placid lethargy of the barges, seemingly immune to waves, that hardly seemed to move at all.

They hid out in a culvert to wait for dark, Chirp and the bear at one end and Mugsy at the other. The bear lay quietly, licking his shoulder now and then out of habit. The wound had furred over except for one patch of pinkish skin, and the animal no longer limped. Chirp reached out and touched the place where the wound had been, and the bear licked his hand with his long pink tongue as though pleased by the attention.

"You're takin' an awful chance," Mugsy said from the other end of the culvert. "That bear hasn't eaten all day."

"Not so doggone loud," Chirp said. "Somebody

might hear you!" He gave Mr. Beans a hug, burying his face in the soft fur of the animal's neck.

Lights twinkled like jewels as they left their hiding place. For some time they moved downstream along the brushy bank of the river, edging around dimly lit docks where barges and tugboats nodded like resting gulls awaiting morning.

Ahead of them, rising and falling gently with passing wakes, was a large raft made of gray, splintered planks atop rusted steel barrels. The wood smelled of diesel oil, tar, and fish. Mr. Beans clambered out on the flimsy structure and sniffed about for food.

At one end of the raft was a massive tiller, indicating that the raft, if towed, might have found occasional use as a fishing platform, or for transporting fuel to waiting barges.

"Just what we need!" Chirp whispered. "Nobody's even going to miss this old wreck."

"What are you doing?" Mugsy questioned as Chirp took out his obsidian blade and began sawing the rotten old mooring ropes in two. "I'm not riding on that old piece of junk. I can't swim!"

"Then stay here in Oregon!" Chirp snapped. He tethered the bear to the center of the raft by the leash, took a piece of plank, and pushed off. Mugsy leaped on at the last moment, sending jets of water squirting through cracks in the floor. Grasping the rudder, Chirp let the current sweep them out into the river.

"Be careful," Mugsy whined. "That water's cold and I'm getting soaked. I want to go back!"

Beyond them in the moonlight, a giant sturgeon rose and swam upstream, its knobby back exposed like an overturned canoe. "What's that?" Mugsy breathed. "It's a sea monster! It'll get us for sure!"

"Oh g'wan," Chirp said. "It's just an old sturgeon. I've heard the Columbia and Snake are full of them. Comes any closer, I'll rap it on the noggin with a plank and we'll have sturgeon steak." Chirp sounded braver than he really felt.

Pushed by a tug, a barge crept past them, heading upriver. A sailor's voice cursed them in the darkness. "Hey, you idjits. Whar's your runnin' lights?"

Chirp thrust hard on the rudder, letting the current sweep them straight downstream, and missed the huge barge by inches. But the experience sobered him. Once the barge lights had disappeared into the darkness, he kept a good watch for other craft, but the moon had vanished behind clouds and too often they were engulfed in blackness as thick as ink, which made it seem that they were now the only ones on the river.

Then the big moon came out from behind the clouds again and made a golden pathway across the water. "Look at that, Mr. Beans," Chirp said, ignoring Mugsy. "No matter which way we sail, the moon's reflection always comes right to us."

The river was swifter now. By holding the rudder just right against the current, they were thrusting forward, making some progress, covering a good hundred feet across the river for every three hundred they were swept downstream. Chirp was elated. "Look at us go!" he laughed. "We'll make it across this old river yet." He could see a few scattered lights twinkling along the Washington shore, but nothing to indicate a town.

They were in the middle of the Columbia when it happened. Chirp heard the faint plash of leaping fish, and suddenly, they were in the middle of a school. There were huge boils all around them and flashes of silver in the moonlight as the fish rolled and splashed. A night wind threw a shower of spray into their faces.

Chirp saw the danger immediately. "Mr. Beans!" he cried out. "Forget the fish! Stay where you are!"

But the bear was on his feet, straining toward the food source. Weakened and soggy with water, the leash rope parted, and suddenly the animal was batting at fish from the edge of the platform. Now the raft began to tip slowly under his heavy weight.

The Indian boy had a glimpse of Mugsy rising higher and higher into the air behind him as the edge of the raft rose. Chirp lost his grip on the heavy tiller; the raft overturned with a crash and was gone. The boys and the grizzly bear were swept away in a churn of water.

"Help me!" Mugsy screamed. "Chirp! Help me!"

Chirp tried to swim toward Mugsy but the currents dragged him down. Coughing and sputtering, he got his head back above water and sucked in some air. Frightened fish bumped his legs. He groped for Mugsy, caught the back of his shirt, and held on, trying to stay behind the screaming boy. Pulling Mugsy toward him and keeping out of reach of his flailing arms, Chirp swam for them both. Mugsy sputtered and whined for help. As long as Chirp could hear him, he knew Mugsy's head was above water.

"Grab onto Mr. Beans!" he commanded. "Come here, big bear. Come help us! Please!"

The current was sweeping the bear away from them, but suddenly the animal began to swim. He turned in a long circle and came up current, paddling hard. Chirp kicked wildly and pulled the flailing boy into the bear's path. The great claws tore at their clothes as the massive animal reached their side.

"Grab on, Mugsy!"

Blindly the boy seized the bear around the neck, but Chirp pulled his arm away. "Don't choke him!" he commanded. "Grab yourself a handful of back hair and let Mr. Beans tow you through the water!"

Mugsy seemed to understand, and the bear turned ponderously against the chop and began to swim slowly, evenly, toward the far shore, towing the two boys behind him.

Sixteen

THE BOYS LAY like a couple of driftwood logs, half in and half out of the water. Mr. Beans shook himself mightily, drenching them with spray, but neither boy could get any wetter. The bear still had those fish on his mind and swam back out into the river to find them. Chirp could hear him splashing in the shallows, and the animal did not return until he had a big fish crosswise in his mouth. He lay on the bank near the boys, devoured his catch, then sniffed the ground eagerly for any morsel he might have missed.

"You'd better level with me, Mugsy," Chirp said. "You don't fool me one bit. Your old man was waiting for us at the ferry dock, ready to grab the pickup and trailer as it docked, and haul Mr. Beans off into the Washington backcountry and shoot him, wasn't he?"

Mugsy turned his face away, but his body was wracked with sobs. Chirp knew he had hit upon the truth. He stumbled to his feet, staggered to a log, and unlaced his boots, pouring out water and sand first from one boot, then the other. He took off his shirt, doubled it around a sapling, and twisted the water out of it. He was through with the white boy and did not care if Mugsy got warm or not.

It was too dark to travel now. Chirp lay down beside a driftwood log to wait, and the night hours seemed longer than any he had ever experienced. When the faint light of dawn appeared, he saw a shack not far away in the willows. Its windows were bird busted and the front door was missing. But it was a place to get out of the wind.

"You!" he said, prodding the older boy with his toe. "Go find your old man and tell him where we are. Let him come shoot this poor grizzly bear if he can. But let him shoot me first, because I am willing to die for an animal that has saved my life and been my true friend."

"Chirp! Chirp! I don't know where he is. You were right; he was waitin' for us to cross on the ferry. It was his idea to load the bear in the trailer and head north on some back road where the law wouldn't be watchin' every move. Once the ferry landed with that bear, he planned to take over and drive the bear back into the hills."

"But where is he now?" Chirp demanded.

"Chirp, I swear to you. I don't know."

Mugsy had just pulled himself to his knees

when Chirp stiffened, suddenly alert. In the distance he heard sounds, the sharp rattle of a pickup truck, tires crushing railroad ballast, the pound of a loose spring as a wheel hit a rock.

He threw his shirt over his shoulders, grabbed the rest of his clothes, and jerked Mugsy to his feet. "Quick!" he snapped. "There's a car coming. Head for that old shack. Come on, Mr. Beans!"

Still dripping water, the bear left a wet trail as he ambled after the boys. The door frame squeaked as the bear squeezed through. The dimness inside was lit only by a pale shaft of morning light entering through a hole in the wall where a window had been.

The grizzly sniffed the air and began tearing into a pile of sticks, papers, and tin cans. A pack rat fled the assault on his nest, scampered up the wall, and peered down at them from a sagging rafter before escaping through a gap in the roof. "Be quiet," Chirp whispered to the bear, scratching his shaggy neck to distract him.

The sound of the motor ceased and was followed by the soft click of a car door being carefully closed; then they heard the faint crunch of crushed rock as someone strolled along the railroad track.

As they waited, the bear lay down in one corner of the shack, licking his paws. "Please, Mr. Beans. Don't even move!" Chirp whispered. As if to defy him, the bear's stomach complained in hunger, sounding like distant thunder.

The pack rat came back through the hole in the roof, then departed again when he saw them. Through an empty window, Chirp could see across the water. He watched scattered clouds scudding over soft yellow hills on the Oregon side of the river.

Try as he might, Chirp could see no sign of the man who had driven up, and his vehicle was hidden by a string of boxcars on the adjacent siding. Somewhere in the brush beside the old ruin of a shack, he heard blackbirds scolding and the voices of the river currents as they boiled and eddied their way toward the Pacific.

Mugsy sat alone in one corner of the shack, pretending to be asleep, but twice Chirp caught him glancing out the door, looking and listening as though he expected someone.

That last gas station in Oregon. Mugsy had taken his own good time paying for the gasoline while Chirp sat in the pickup. Chirp was pretty sure the boy had telephoned his father to let him know they were approaching the Columbia and would take the ferry as planned.

The events of the night had been so unexpected, Chirp thought that even Mr. Flanigan could not have predicted them. The man could make some guesses, but he probably didn't know where they were.

There was no sound of anyone along the track. Chirp wondered if he could risk slipping out of the shack to look beyond the railroad cars and see if there was still a car parked there.

Out of the corner of his eye, he saw Mugsy stiffen and go ghastly pale. Chirp followed his startled glance out the doorway, and there in full view stood Mr. Flanigan, his rifle up and ready, staring at the hut.

Chirp pulled a sharp stick from the pack rat's nest and stood between the bear and the door, ready to defend the animal with his life. He glared at the friend who had betrayed him.

Mugsy shot past him out the door, talking a blue streak. "Dad! Dad! I'm here! Don't let Chirp and that damn bear get away! We crossed the river last night on a raft and it tipped over. I stayed with the raft, thank God, and got ashore. They were swept downstream but I'm sure they didn't get very far. I think Chirp broke his leg! And the bear's wound broke open and he couldn't swim a lick. I guess all you'll find of him is a carcass washed up on some old sandbar."

Chirp heard two car doors slam. The engine raced and tires squealed as Mugsy and his father sped down the service road that shared the riverbank with the railroad tracks.

"Quick, Mr. Beans," Chirp exclaimed. "Let's get out of here in case Mr. Flanigan ever finds out our pal Mugsy was lying!"

Seventeen

CHIRP WAS DRYING HIS SHIRT on a bush when the next train came rumbling past, moving slowly eastward past the empty boxcars parked on the siding. Steam from the locomotive filled the little glade like dancing ghosts. Once the last car had cleared the switch, the train stopped, and freight cars bumped together until all the slack was out of the couplings. A man dropped off the caboose to throw the switch, then signaled the engineer to reverse. The train gradually moved back along the spur until, with a bang of bumping couplers, the empties became part of the train. Slowly the big steam locomotive began to creep forward, pulling the cars onto the main line.

"C'mon, Mr. Beans," Chirp shouted above the din. "You're looking at our free ticket to Idaho!"

The bear was frightened by the train and seemed to sense Chirp's anxiety, but he followed as though he were more afraid of being left behind. At the edge of the thickets of willow and alder brush, Chirp put on his shirt, slipped his pack over his shoulders, and glanced up the tracks at the switchman who stood putting a heavy padlock on the switch.

Chirp took his one remaining can of sardines from his jacket pocket and shook it at the bear. "Hurry up, Mr. Beans," he called and sprinted for an open boxcar, while the bear followed like a big brown shadow. Had the railroad man chanced to look back, he would have seen a boy and a huge grizzly bear clambering into his train.

Chirp glanced back along the cars in time to see the switchman climb aboard. It seemed to Chirp that the train took forever to start again, but soon the locomotive began to chuff and puff, and car by car the wheels began to move and pick up speed. As the train rumbled and swayed, they headed eastward at last up the great gorge of the Columbia.

Having licked the can of sardines clean and pushed it across the floor of the car with his nose until it finally dropped through the open door, Mr. Beans seemed hungrier than ever and sat up on his haunches, swaying with every lurch of the car, begging for food.

"You've got to be patient, Old Bear. We're fresh out of grub and won't be able to scrounge off the land until we get off. But at least we're headed where we want to go. Uncle Frank, he'd be pretty excited to know we'd gotten this close to Idaho!"

The bear listened to Chirp's voice as if he

were trying hard to understand, then plunked down beside the boy and began to snooze. Whenever the freight train stopped on sidings to let westbound trains slide past, Mr. Beans opened his eyes briefly, then resumed his dreams when the thunder had passed. Chirp wished he could relax like the bear.

The train spent most of the next night parked in a huge railroad yard near a large city. Toward dawn workers came to service the train, piling fresh coal into the tender and adding water for the boiler. Chirp could hear the clank of steel as car by car, men checked the bearing boxes on each car. Some of the empties were shunted off and left on sidings, bound for other destinations, but luckily, Chirp's car stayed with the train. Just before dawn they headed out of the yard.

As the cars started to pick up speed, there was a thud by the open door of Chirp's car and the clank of metal as a heavy sack skidded across the floor. Chirp was startled by a grunt as a man pulled himself into the car and crawled toward the far wall.

Chirp smelled the odor of cheap wine and fetid clothes as the figure rose unsteadily to his feet, then fell down again, cursing.

Chirp said nothing, but leaned back against the bear. In the gloom the boy could see that the man was powerfully built. Chirp knew he would have his hands full if the hobo attacked. He wondered if he had gotten rid of Mr. Flanigan only to inherit something worse.

He watched as the dim figure fiddled with his sack of possessions, then pulled something out and dropped it in the darkness. It was metal, and Chirp hoped it wasn't a gun.

There was a tearing sound and the hiss of a can being stabbed open with a knife. The smell of pork and beans wafted through the car. Mr. Beans stirred in his slumber but did not wake.

Suddenly the man sensed their presence. "Who the hell's there? What you doin' in my car?"

The beam of a flashlight played across Chirp's face, and a powerful hand shot out to grasp him by the throat.

"Lemme go!" Chirp screamed. He struck with his fists, but the hobo only cursed in rage and twisted his fingers in the thong about the boy's neck.

Chirp gasped for breath; the cord cut deeply into his flesh. He managed to whirl away and suddenly, mercifully, the cord broke and the man tumbled backwards with Chirp's medicine bag in his hand.

"Mr. Beans!" Chirp screamed, sucking in air. "Help! Help!"

The great bear struggled with sleep but came awake, sniffing the air. The odor of wine and baked beans pervaded the car, and the hungry animal lurched abruptly to his feet and rose high over the frightened tramp in his search for food.

"Yiiiiii!" screamed the man as he leaped for the door of the boxcar. The train was thundering fast when the man flung himself out into the darkness and was gone, leaving his sack of possessions behind.

By the time daylight made slow sense of the railroad car, the bear had scattered the contents of the sack over the floor and gobbled up anything unprotected by a can. Somehow the animal had managed to chew the cap from a gallon of muscatel wine and lapped up the spilled contents. The bear now smelled as bad as the hobo, and Chirp recoiled from his breath.

Frantically the boy searched the car for his medicine bag and the map, his only link to Uncle Frank. On his hands and knees, he groped in the shadows, feeling every inch of the darkened corners. Then suddenly, as he was about to give up, his hands closed on the familiar buckskin sack. He sagged back, exhausted, against the wall of the car, holding the sack close to his heart.

The bear sat in the middle of the floor, looking absently out over the passing countryside and rolling a can of pork and beans on the splintered floor with one big paw. Once he had his wind back, Chirp gathered the rest of the canned goods and placed them in his pack for future emergencies, while the bear, deprived of his playthings, retreated to a far corner to sleep off the effects of the wine.

That afternoon their future was decided for them when the empty boxcars were shunted off to a siding and left in the hot sun. The train blew a lonely good-bye at a road crossing and vanished around a bend in the track.

To the south, through one door of the boxcar,

Chirp saw the rectangular geometrics of potato fields that were soon to make Idaho famous, and a billboard along the neighboring highway touted Idaho produce as the best in the world. North of them, through the other door, stretched a forest of tall, stately aspens, which merged with a dark green sea of pines, that, in turn, swept on to the very threshold of towering mountains in the distance.

The boy leaped down from the boxcar and hoisted his pack. "Come on, Mr. Beans!" he called out excitedly. He moved across the heavy ballast on the shoulder of the track, while the bear descended from the car backwards, feeling for the ground with first one hind foot, then the other, until he finally made contact. In a small, wet meadow shaded by aspens, bear and boy gathered dandelion greens, and it was only when their hunger pangs had ceased that the pair headed for higher country.

Unencumbered by Mugsy and his complaining ways, they made good time, pausing to rest only when the bear found an infestation of grasshoppers and could not be distracted from them.

It didn't make much sense to Chirp that such a huge animal would bother chasing these tiny insects, but the bear would slap down a paw with enough force to fell an ox, then spend valuable time licking up whatever he had managed to crush.

The two found a little moraine lake, scooped out by glaciers during an ice age, nestled between two hills. Here they bathed and rested, gorging themselves on big orange salmonberries.

A black bear sought to join them in the feast, but when Mr. Beans stood on his hind legs and peered at the encroacher, the other bear woofed and departed up over the nearest ridge.

Trout dimpled the silver mirror of the lake, but Chirp had no way of catching them. The big bear crashed into the water, destroying the calm, and tried to capture a fish, but he finally swam in, frustrated, looking back over his shoulder as though he resented the trout for making a fool of him. Chirp moved away from the wet bear, but the animal still drenched him with a spray of water.

Almost out of habit, Chirp doubled back on his tracks, afraid that someone might stumble upon their footprints. As long as they remained in semi-civilized country, Chirp knew that sooner or later they might come face-to-face with a rancher or camper and the land would quickly be abuzz with the story of a boy and a grizzly bear traveling together toward the mountains.

No matter how hard Chirp tried to hide their tracks, the bear ignored caution and left a trail of destruction in his wake: rotten logs ripped open for pale, fat boreworm grubs; cinnamon hairs on barbed wire fences; berry bushes stripped of fruit by raking claws; orchard trees with broken branches where the bear had found that the easy way to reach that certain cluster of fruit was to knock the entire branch down; snorting, bug-eyed horses; and great manlike footprints in streamside mud.

Under cover of darkness, the boy scouted from

the ridges and planned the next day's journey by mapping the lights of distant ranch houses. He learned the position of roads as car headlights betrayed their routes. The larger roads he avoided completely or at least crossed only at night.

One morning they skirted a vast irrigated meadow surrounded by groves of towering aspens. Chirp paused to wonder at the beauty of it all. There were wetlands blue as lakes with camas blossoms, and the boy remembered his Uncle Frank telling him that beneath each stalk was a large bulb that could be roasted and eaten like candy. Indians had fought wars over the camas fields, but the white man's hogs had come in and rooted out most of the plants. Now Chirp sat and listened. From the meadows came the hum of bees and the fragrance of blossoming clover.

But there were humans there, too, men whose rifles showed in the back windows of their pickup trucks. Tiny, harmless-looking figures in the distance, driving two-horse mowers, rakes, and sweeps, making huge bread loaves of hay for winter. Men who would eagerly pause in the midst of haying operations to hunt down a grizzly bear.

Ahead of them at last were towering mountains where there were no lights at night, the land Uncle Frank loved, a vast island in the middle of Idaho that no railroad or highway dared challenge. One minute the boy and the bear could look back at distant ranches, the next they were swallowed up by a jagged moonscape of rock where there was as much travel up and down as forward. It was as though they had retreated ten thousand years back in time.

It was hard to follow the thin map of parchment that Uncle Frank had made for him. Vital landmarks were obscured by folds and creases in the weasel hide. Sometimes he wasted miles of travel when he misread the map.

One day, following Uncle Frank's directions, Chirp climbed with the bear to a vast forested plateau rich with wildflowers, where towering ponderosa pines were interspersed with hardwoods. And right where the parchment showed it to be, Chirp found a strange cliff, at the base of which were the remains of an Indian village.

Circles of brightly colored rocks lay partly buried in the earth where early people had anchored down their tipi liners against the wind, and left those rings for others when they eventually broke camp and moved on, taking their tipis with them.

On the face of the cliff, an ancient people had left their history thousands of years before. Using rock hammers and sharp tines of deer antlers, those early artists pecked in the richness of their world. Here mountain goats, deer, bison, antelope, grizzly bears, eagles, and woolly mammoths graced the walls. There a tiny birdlike hunter documented his success by tracing not only the snake-like wanderings of his endeavor but the tracks of his quarry on the rock, tracks that came to an abrupt end as they did in real life when the hunter made his kill. That early hunter left the gift of his adventure for those who would follow him in time.

Standing near those petroglyphs, Chirp felt a strong link with those who had gone before. "Sometime," Uncle Frank had said, "you will come to appreciate the privilege of being born Indian, and you will come to understand that you are part of a history that stretches back thousands of years."

As though sensing the boy's mood, the great grizzly came to stand beside him and touched his brown cheek with a moist nose. To Chirp it was as though a bear had stepped down from the rock art on the wall to join him and help him on his way.

Eighteen

By now Chirp had acquired a certain proficiency in reading Uncle Frank's map. When Uncle Frank marked a mountain, he meant a BIG mountain. When he marked a river, he meant a BIG river. When he marked a canyon, he meant a BIG canyon. It was vital not to jump to conclusions and say that the hill you saw before you was the mountain the old Indian had marked on the parchment. Chirp learned that if he gave it another day or two of travel, he would suddenly come to a mountain that had to be THE mountain.

One thing Uncle Frank had not counted on was that Chirp would be traveling with a grizzly bear when he chose to use the map and could not risk running into other travelers.

Once, they descended a canyon Chirp knew was the middle fork of the Salmon, hoping to cross the silvery river they saw far below, only to find on close inspection that the river was a raging torrent and there was no possibility of getting to the other side. Patiently he climbed back to the heights, noticing what had escaped him before—that the crossing Uncle Frank had marked was probably thirty miles farther north. They followed along the shoulders of the canyon where the going was easier, peering occasionally down into the gorge at mile after mile of booming rapids.

The mountains became more numerous. At night they rose as a heavy, jagged blackness against the starry sky. Even with a full moon, it was dangerous to travel, and so the boy chose to do his sleeping at night, arising in the chill as first light stole over the dragon's teeth of encircling peaks.

On his parchment map, the trail showed as a series of tiny horseshoes, hardly more than dots, crossing the river and proceeding up the other side. The ruggedness of the land and its peaks was indicated by a number of X's. Chirp felt tingles up his spine as he came over a ridge and found a trail right where there should be one. The path was well worn, made by shod horses, not mustangs, and seemed to lead to the river bottom.

"We'll have to take a chance on not meeting anyone," Chirp said aloud to the bear. "Horses and grizzlies don't mix!"

Mr. Beans sniffed briefly at the tracks, then followed Chirp down the trail.

At the bottom was an abandoned homestead. A John Deere wheel tractor stood off-balance with a flat tire and ready to give in to an attack of rust. Chirp guessed that the tractor had been broken down into parts and brought in by pack animals, then reassembled on the spot. At the head of the orchard stood an old log house, its roof caved in by time and winter snows.

Chirp searched the orchard for fruit, but the trees had succumbed to neglect and porcupine damage. What few early apples he could find were deformed by insects. There were ashes along the stream where someone had camped some time before and tethered a pack string for the night, but no recent sign to cause him alarm.

Following the trail upstream from the homestead, the boy rounded a bend to find a ferry spanning the torrent. It was little more than a raft attached by cables and hand winches to stout trees on the shore. From the tracks Chirp figured that the outfitter had tied up his horses and taken them one at a time across the ferry. That done, he had headed east up the trail.

He coaxed the bear onto the raft and secured him firmly in the middle. Then, by feeding slack into the left cable and tightening the right, he let the current sweep the raft across the stream.

The trail climbed steeply, and soon the ferry had disappeared behind a bend in the river. Ahead of them a herd of cow elk and their calves clattered over rocky escarpments and were gone before the boy could get a look at them. Soon Chirp and the bear moved out onto a vast plateau covered with pines. The trail continued on its eastward course, and Chirp was relieved to see that the map indicated he should leave the track at this point and follow the edge of the plateau in a northeasterly direction.

For a mile or so, Chirp followed a faint path skirting a marsh, then fought his way through thickets until he came back onto his own trail. He consulted the map again but the lines were obliterated by the folds in the parchment. He tried the trail again, skirting the thickets, and this time emerged onto a green meadow more beautiful than any he had seen before. He sat down on a rotten log to rest while the bear moved off to explore the grassland.

From a hole high in a decaying aspen beside the wet meadow came the raucous calling of young woodpeckers. The boy caught a flash of powdery blue from a rotting stump out in the meadow, as a mountain bluebird flew down to seize a grasshopper and returned to its perch. Disturbed by the bear, a covey of blue grouse exploded under Mr. Beans' feet and scaled away to safety, while others watched calmly enough from neighboring rocks as though they had no reason to fear.

High above them a pair of golden eagles soared, feeling out the warm thermals rising from the canyon walls, rising as though lifted by an unseen giant hand until they were specks in the brilliant blue and the boy could look at them no longer without his eyes brimming with tears.

"Look at this place, Mr. Beans! I never saw a

place more beautiful! It's as though my ancestors knew of this place and have been directing our steps every inch of the way. Or maybe Uncle Frank was in on it. You suppose?"

The great bear turned at the sound of the boy's excitement and peered back at him from eyes set deep in heavy fur, then plunked down in the lush, wet meadow grass as though waiting for the boy to catch up.

Chirp rushed to the bear and threw his arms around the big animal's neck. "This is home, Mr. Beans! This is the place I promised you! Maybe there aren't any grizzlies around, but there could be. Look at the beaver dams over there in that stream! Betcha there could be monstrous trout in them. Plenty of elk droppings here in the meadow, and over by those pines must be a dozen white-tailed deer."

Suddenly the big bear gave a woof of alarm, rising quickly to his feet. He stood on his hind legs, the better to see across the meadow. A light breeze played with the long, yellow guard hairs along his hump. Chirp followed the animal's gaze but saw nothing.

Then came a roll like distant thunder, and a band of wild horses broke from a grove of aspen and trotted toward them, heads high, ears perked forward, nostrils flared to drink the wind. Eyes bulging, they stopped to stare, then circled downwind to establish the identity of these intruders to their world.

"Counting foals, must be thirty head!" Chirp

breathed. "I wonder if Uncle Frank knows about them. He'd almost rather run horses than pan for gold."

There were grullas the color of soft blue velvet with zebra stripes on their forelegs. There were sorrels with blaze faces, their white stockings flashing as they splashed through a slough and emerged dripping on the other side. There were bays, blacks, cremellos and a scattering of paints that looked like Indian ponies of long ago.

The paint stallion laid back its ears and seemed ready to challenge the bear, but a lead mare caught their scent, snorted, and thundered off. Soon the herd was only a ghost of dust lingering along the rocky headland above the plateau as the mustangs headed for higher country where they felt more secure.

For a time Chirp worked with a digging stick and unearthed a mess of camas bulbs to roast for supper, then trapped some fine trout in the shallows below a beaver dam. Some of the fish he dressed out, split down the middle, then hung to dry in a dead juniper tree, high enough that Mr. Beans could not reach them.

Beaver were already out swimming in their ponds when the boy decided to stop fishing and seek shelter for the night. While the bear wandered off to chase flightless young ducks in the marsh grass, Chirp climbed through a jumble of rocks strewn down from towering rimrocks by time. There the boy settled in and sat watching the sun disappear behind the mountains.

Nineteen

CHIRP SAT ON SOME ROCKS, munching fresh greens and eating handfuls of huckleberries he had picked on the site of an old burn. Mr. Beans had found a berry patch of his own and was happily stuffing himself with fruit. The boy was relieved to be here in the Idaho wilderness at last, but he was frustrated, too. The big lava cone above him showed on the map, but beyond that the parchment that had brought him this far no longer seemed to be of use to him. To survive, he had to find his Uncle Frank, but he was slowly being overpowered by the immensity of this land.

He took the map out of his medicine bag again and spread it carefully on his knees. As he did so, the arrowhead and the three little sticks fell from the leather sack. He thought that maybe the sticks could be used to tell the future and cast them repeatedly on the ground, but there was no consistency to the way they fell. Then, as he picked them up again, he noticed that one end of each stick was sharpened as though it was meant to pierce something.

A gray jay flew down and sat on a branch close by, hoping for a handout. Usually he would have relished the bird's company, but now he waved the jay away. He was fascinated by the sticks, yet puzzled by them.

Chirp looked again at the map. Uncle Frank would not have lured him into the wilderness with the map had he not intended him to find the cabin. Yet there was only one dot left on the map, and that was in the middle of a big empty space. The old man had purposely drawn a map that was hard to follow. "Maybe," Chirp thought, "maybe I'm wrong to think the sticks have magic powers. Maybe they are just sticks, sharpened to stick through something. Something like the parchment. There are three of them. One perhaps for my past position, one for the present, and one for the future."

He knelt in the sand and stretched out the fragile skin. He was high enough on a ridge to be able to look back on his trail of previous days. Excited now, he lined up the distant plateau where he had crossed the Middle Fork of the Salmon and pushed one of the sharpened sticks through the parchment into the ground. He rotated the map until the trail aligned exactly with the next known point, where he knelt now in the shadow of the volcanic cone.

He pushed the second stick into place. Hands trembling with excitement, he pushed the third stick through the last dot on the weasel skin.

He realized suddenly that the map Uncle Frank had made for him had not been carelessly drawn from memory on some rough-hewn cabin table but sketched on the trail as he traveled it. Chirp now knew in which direction the cabin lay, and by comparison with previous sections, he had a fair idea of how far it was across the empty spot on the map.

By sighting over the sharpened sticks on the parchment, he was able to establish his line of travel. The cabin must be at the base of the flat-topped mesa he could see in the distance, and the boy figured he had eight more miles to go.

Calling the bear, he moved off, keeping his eyes on the mesa as he walked and growing more excited with each passing mile.

He was relieved when he saw a cabin at the end of a small meadow. It was so hemmed in by pines that Chirp almost passed by without seeing it. Behind the cabin a gentle, brushy slope gave way to towering rimrocks. It was exactly the kind of cabin Uncle Frank would have built for himself in a land where there was no neighborhood hardware store.

Instead of being sawed, each log had been carefully flattened with an adze on four sides, and the corners were painstakingly notched to fit. The cracks were filled with sphagnum moss and sealed with clay. A blanket of decaying pine needles covered the split-shake roof.

"Hey, Uncle Frank! You there?" Chirp's voice echoed from the rims and sent a pair of black-and-white magpies fleeing over the treetops. The boy had a sinking feeling that no one had been around for quite some time.

The hand-hewn planks on the front porch creaked under his weight, and the bent horseshoe hinges on the door squealed like a dog-bit pig as he pulled open the door.

The place was a shambles. Pack rats had built a huge nest of sticks and pine cones on top of the sheepherder stove. There was a long, plank table, and around it were benches stacked with the tattered and worn Western magazines Uncle Frank loved. On the wall was a yellowed photograph of Sacajawea, the Indian woman who had been an interpreter for western explorers.

That Uncle Frank had intended to return was evidenced by his 30-30 carbine on the wall, hanging in its worn cowhide saddle scabbard; the precise piles of firewood, carefully split and stacked; and the stocks of food tightly sealed in blue Mason jars. There was a cupboard lined with zinc to prevent rodent incursions. Inside, clean and neatly folded, were gray-wool military blankets and flannel sheets.

Hanging from wooden pegs driven into the wall were the tools of a miner's trade: shovels, picks, rock hammers, pry-bars, and gold pans. All showed signs of heavy wear, testimony to the hard labors of a man who hated to be idle. A pack rat was in residence. For a moment it paused to look down from a rafter in big-eyed wonder. There was a smell of juniper in the air, a pack rat trademark; Chirp wondered that the pretty brown-and-white animal could be so messy.

In front of the stove was a chair of sorts, the kind of seat cowboys once whittled by necessity out of rough boards and left around ranch bunkhouses when they moved on.

He was worried about Uncle Frank and wondered what had happened to him. The last entry on the 1940 wall calendar had been made on May third, nearly three months ago, and was crudely printed with the stub of a pencil hanging from a string. "Grizzly stole the last of my venison."

Chirp recognized Uncle Frank's scrawl.

Tired of traveling, and intrigued by the thought of good food, Chirp felt the sudden urge to nest. It seemed like his cabin now since he had worked so hard to get here. He cut some willow shoots and wired them together into a crude broom. Taking a flat shovel from the wall, he swept the floor and scattered the pack rat's debris across the meadow.

When he had finished cleaning, he felt better. Mr. Beans was still far up on the hillside, foraging for berries. He called the bear, wanting to show off the clean cabin, but the animal was too busy doing bear things to crave human company. With each day that passed, the grizzly was becoming more independent, and the boy hoped the animal would leave him one day for a life in the wild.

He liked to think that Uncle Frank was merely

off prospecting and would come back to the cabin soon, but deep within the boy was a gnawing dread that the old man had met with an accident, and no one would ever know what had happened to him. The life of a lonely prospector was dangerous, particularly for those lucky enough to make a strike. There were always bad folks who were ready to separate a miner from his gold.

Chirp was sitting on the front porch when Mr. Beans came down off the hill. He licked the Indian boy's hand as though he craved salt. The boy scratched the bear's ears, then, in a burst of happiness, began whistling a polka. The bear stood up on his hind legs and whirled round and round with the music. Still whistling, the boy stood up and danced until he was dizzy and had to hold onto one of the porch uprights to keep from falling.

Evening was almost upon them when he saw the wild grizzly. For a moment Chirp thought Mr. Beans had slipped away and was heading out to forage, but when he glanced around the corner of the cabin, he saw his friend stretched out beside the wall, sound asleep.

The wild bear spent a few minutes sniffing at the pack rat debris, then ambled over to a seep spring along the edge of the meadow. He drank slowly, turned, and was gone into the thickets as though he had never been there.

"You missed it, Mr. Beans! You missed seeing a real wild grizzly. First one I ever saw in my whole life and you slept through the whole thing."

Chirp took Mr. Beans for a stroll along the meadow where the wild bear had crossed, hoping that the tame bear might show some excitement. But Mr. Beans only sniffed the huge tracks and moved on.

Chirp followed the tracks for a mile or so through the pines, moving warily, wanting to make sure the wild animal had left the area. He lost the tracks on the talus slopes beneath the rims that edged the valley. He was not at all interested in meeting a wild bear face-to-face. From now on he would have to be more cautious.

The sun was just going down as they returned to the cabin. Chirp paused at the door for a moment, thinking how careless he had been to leave the door to the cabin wide open so that bears and porcupines could enter at will. It was only after he had built a fire in the stove and started to make some biscuits that he happened to look at the wall across from the stove. The rifle that had been hanging there in its scabbard was gone!

Twenty

SUDDENLY, THE CABIN, which had seemed his place of refuge, felt more like a trap. He was caught inside, a prisoner of someone unknown. Maybe it was Uncle Frank out there, but what if it wasn't? Maybe someone had just happened by and found the cabin empty, stolen the rifle, and was now putting as much distance as possible between them. More likely the person was still outside in the darkness, waiting in complete control, armed with Uncle Frank's 30-30 carbine.

He wished Mr. Beans had come in with him, but the bear had gone down across the meadow at dusk, maybe to drink from the spring. He opened the door a crack and listened carefully to the night sounds. A horned owl shrieked, and somewhere from afar a whippoorwill was calling. Bats squeaked about the eaves.

What if Uncle Frank had come back to his cabin and mistaken him for someone wanting to rob him of his gold? The old Indian hadn't seen him in a while. In that time Chirp had shot up a couple of feet.

Minutes dragged by. The moon came out from behind a cloud and bathed the meadow in soft light. There was the faint booming of thunder far to the west and flickerings of chain lightning. The cabin seemed more and more oppressive.

Inch by inch he opened the door, hoping the rusty hinges wouldn't give him away. He waited until the moon went behind a cloud and slipped out, feeling better when he had gained the safety of the thickets along the meadow. Sitting quietly, he analyzed each night sound. In the distance a family of coyotes was learning to howl; close by, almost at the boy's feet, leaves rustled with mice. Higher on the rims, a night bird fluttered into darkness, looking for a safer perch.

He took a biscuit from his pocket and nibbled at it, but it seemed dry and tasteless and he tossed it aside. With his back to a pile of rocks, he lay back and tried to rest. The moon seemed to take forever to cross the sky. He missed Mr. Beans and wondered if he was still splashing around down by the spring.

He awoke to scraping sounds nearby. Daylight already. Dimly he saw Mr. Beans sitting a few feet downslope, working the soil with one big paw where Chirp had tossed food scraps into the darkness. A light breeze played across the brown and yellow hairs on the bear's coat. Chirp thought he had never seen Mr. Beans looking so big and healthy, or noticed before just how massive was the hump on his shoulders. With one giant foot, the grizzly scratched the side of his neck, and Chirp marveled at how polished the bear's claws had become from digging and walking miles through dusty, abrasive grasses.

Lying still, he planned his day. He would stay hidden on the hillside where he would have a clear view of the cabin and the surrounding country and maybe get a good look at the person who had taken the gun. Right now he was thirsty and thought he could get to the spring through the thickets without exposing himself to whoever might be watching.

He tied his boots and stretched, then rose and walked toward Mr. Beans to give him a hug. The bear still sat looking down the hillside; as Chirp approached, the animal tucked in his jaw and began grooming his chest.

"Good morn—!" Chirp had just started the sentence and stretched out an arm to stroke the animal when the big grizzly let out a startled woof and whirled, raking the astonished boy on the chest with one lightning strike of a paw.

"Mr. Beans!" Chirp screamed, then recoiled in terror when he saw that it was not Mr. Beans at all.

He scrambled up and tried to climb the pile of rocks, but the bear grabbed the boy's boot in his teeth and attempted to drag him back.

Suddenly, from up on the rimrock, a fusillade of shots broke out. The bear leaped high as though stung, crashed over the jumbles of rock, and was gone.

"Don't shoot!" Chirp screamed. He heard a rattle of toenails on rock and thought for a moment the grizzly was coming back, but it was only Mr. Beans.

He heard another volley of shots from on high, but Mr. Beans kept coming.

"Don't shoot my pet bear," he shouted again, but his voice seemed less of a shout than a whisper. Mr. Beans ambled over and stood beside him. Chirp's chest hurt but he had to save Mr. Beans. He tried to raise himself and get in front of the bear.

"Lie still, mister!" he heard someone shout. "I'm comin' closer fer a better shot!"

Chirp struggled to his knees. He could see the man now, Uncle Frank himself, sliding down the talus slope on his back, holding the gun up over his head. The boy tried again to call out, but his voice was gone.

There seemed to be only one thing he could do and that was to whistle! He pursed his lips and began a polka. Suddenly Mr. Beans rose up on his hind legs and began to dance!

"What the hell!" Chirp heard Uncle Frank exclaim as he landed on his feet at the bottom of the slope. "A dancin' bear?"

Faster and faster the bear whirled around him. Chirp felt that maybe he had broken a rib, but he forced himself to his feet. Still whistling, he moved in close to the bear and began to pirouette.

"Put the gun away, Uncle Frank," he managed to call out. "Mr. Beans here, he's my friend!"

Twenty-One

WHILE MUGSY WOULD HAVE BEEN a complete basket case, Chirp took his mauling by the wild grizzly silently and well. His ribs ached, and there were huge tooth marks on one boot, but he was able to move down to the cabin on his own power.

Mr. Beans ignored the old Indian, but Uncle Frank could not get used to being that close to a grizzly. He held tight to his rifle when the bear reached out with a giant paw and investigated his long braid, then sniffed the buckskin garments as though the man were a deer in human form.

Still shaken by the events of the morning, Chirp did not feel much like talking, but he did fill Uncle Frank in on how he happened to be traveling with a tame bear.

Chirp had grown attached to the cabin on the

meadow and was disappointed to learn that Uncle Frank didn't call it home. "Aw, it ain't much," he said. "I built that cabin as a line shack, in case I ever got trapped by a storm on my way to and from McCall. Lucky I dropped by to pick up my rifle or I might not have been there to scare off that wild grizzly. It's another fifty, sixty miles on to where I got my tipi."

He looked at the boy and the bear, bemused, and twisted his cap so the beak hung down over one ear. "Whenever you get so you feel like travelin'," he said, "we'll leave this old camp to the pack rats and journey on."

Two days later Chirp was still sore, but impatient to proceed. Soon they left the little valley behind and were headed north across a vast plateau. The old man forged on ahead, chipping away at rocks as he went as though there were a chance for a gold vein in every outcropping.

Behind them came the bear, stopping to tear apart logs for grubs or scalp a piece of sod for rodents.

That night they camped at a spring. Uncle Frank shot a snowshoe rabbit with his rifle, took one of Chirp's pots, and cooked up a delicious stew, which they ate quickly while the bear was off on one of his frequent forays for food. After they had eaten, Uncle Frank made a poultice of some leaves he had gathered along a stream, boiled them, then gently covered the purple bruises on the boy's body where the bear had struck.

"Only place they grow," the old man explained, "or I'd have done this sooner." It seemed to Chirp only moments before the pain eased, and all he could think about was going to sleep.

Now and then he tried to get Uncle Frank to talk about where they were going, but the old man merely grinned and adjusted the beak of his hat. "You'll see," he said, black eyes twinkling. "You'll see."

The next afternoon they passed through a valley where aspen trees grew tall and beaver had dammed up a series of large ponds. Wood ducks rocketed up through the trees and blue herons flew off croaking in alarm. In the mud on the upper margins of the ponds, grizzlies had been taking baths, and Mr. Beans carefully smelled the scents along the edge of the water. He lay down in the mud and rolled and rolled, coating himself until only his eyes showed.

Uncle Frank pointed silently toward a ridge where a big grizzly sow and her cub were eating huckleberries. They left Mr. Beans splashing happily in one of the beaver dams. It was hours later that the bear finally caught up with them. Mr. Beans kept looking back along the trail as though wanting to return to that magical bear playground.

"Maybe one day he will find that bears are more fun to pal with than humans," the old Indian said.

Chirp could tell they were approaching home, for Uncle Frank was getting visibly excited. He kept turning his hat round and round his head and grinning to himself. Chirp was ready to stop; it seemed to him that they had already traveled over a hundred miles.

As they climbed to the top of a steep hill, the old man took the boy by the arm. "Close your eyes," he said, smiling. "Don't open them until I tell you."

He took the boy by the shoulder and guided him forward.

"Now open your eyes," he said as they reached the top of the hill. "Look there and you will see my little tipi!"

Below them lay a small, pretty valley. "I never made a big strike," Uncle Frank said, "but I found enough gold for this."

A neat little whitewashed log house stood at the edge of a stream, and tall straight aspens grew all around. The house, orchard, and garden were surrounded by a white fence. Wash fluttered from a clothesline. There was a woman's touch about the place, and Chirp sensed that Uncle Frank was no longer living alone. Cows grazed in the meadow; horses lazed in the corral; chickens scratched in the barnyard; flowers bloomed in neat rows in a big garden.

Not far from the main house on a little hill was a cabin, its new yellow logs neatly squared with an adze. The little building had a roof of shakes, freshly split. It seemed like a perfect reproduction of Uncle Frank's line cabin.

"I built it for you," the old man said. "I knew that one day you would open the little medicine bag and find the map. It wasn't the best map, but I had faith that eventually you would understand it.

I could not make it easy or others might have come instead." He reached up for the beak of his cap and turned it sideways on his head. "I finished the cabin a month ago. Since then I have been to the line cabin many times and have worn out these hills with my pacing."

"The three sharpened sticks," Chirp said. "It took me a long time to figure out how to use them. And the bird point—I could have interpreted that in a thousand ways."

"The bird point was for luck," the old Indian said. "I found it along the Columbia River when I was a boy. While I carried it, it brought me good fortune. Even after I had given it to you, it brought me the love of a good woman. And now," Uncle Frank smiled, "the little arrowhead has split the wind for you and brought you safely home."

Uncle Frank turned the beak of his hat until it pointed sharply forward. "The bear!" he said. "He was right here behind us when we started talking. Where on earth did that big rascal go?"

There was a moment when all the world seemed to stand silent, then suddenly, all hell broke loose in Uncle Frank's little ranch house. Mr. Beans shot out the door carrying a side of bacon, and right on his tail was a gray-haired Indian lady hitting him on the rump with a broom!